Divine Wedding

Divine Cozy Mystery Series Book 7

Hope Callaghan

hopecallaghan.com

Copyright © 2021
All rights reserved.

Visit my website for new releases and special offers:
hopecallaghan.com

This book is a work of fiction. Although places mentioned may be real, the characters, names and incidents, and all other details are products of the author's imagination and are fictitious. Any resemblance to actual organizations, events, or actual persons, living or dead is purely coincidental.

No part of this publication may be copied, reproduced in any format, by any means, electronic or otherwise, without prior consent from the copyright owner and publisher of this book.

D1738801

i

Acknowledgments

Thank you to these wonderful ladies who help make my books shine - Peggy H., Cindi G., Jean P., Wanda D., Renate P., Alix C. and Sheila G. for taking the time to preview *Divine Wedding,* for the extra sets of eyes and for catching all of my mistakes.

A special THANKS to my reader review team:

Alice, Alta, Amary, Amy, Becky, Brenda, Carolyn, Charlene, Christine, Debbie, Denota, Devan, Diann, Grace, Helen, Jo-Ann, Jean M, Judith, Marilyn, Meg, Megan, Linda, Polina, Rebecca, Rita, Theresa, Valerie and Virginia.

Contents

Cast of Characters

Joanna "Jo" Pepperdine. After suffering a series of heartbreaking events, Jo Pepperdine decides to open a halfway house for recently released female convicts, just outside the small town of Divine, Kansas. She assembles a small team of new friends and employees to make her dream a reality. Along the way, she comes to realize that not only has she given some women a second chance at life, but she's also given herself a new lease on life.

Delta Childress. Delta is Jo's second in command. She and Jo became fast friends after Jo hired her to run the bakeshop and household. Delta is a no-nonsense asset, with a soft spot for the women who are broken, homeless, hopeless and in need of a hand up when they walk through Second Chance's doors. Although Delta isn't keen on becoming involved in the never-ending string of mysteries around town, she finds herself in over her head more often than not.

Raylene Baxter. Raylene is among the first women to come to the farm after being released from Central State Women's Penitentiary. Raylene, a former bond agent/bounty hunter, has a knack for sleuthing out clues and helping Jo catch the bad guys.

Nash Greyson. Nash, Jo's right-hand man, is the calming force in her world of crisis. He's not necessarily on board with Jo and Delta sticking their noses into matters that are better left to the authorities but often finds himself right in the thick of things, rescuing Delta and Jo when circumstances careen out of control.

Gary Stein. While Delta runs the bakeshop and household, and Nash is the all-around-handyman, Gary, a retired farmer, works his magic in Jo's vegetable gardens. A widower, he finds purpose in helping Jo and the farm.

And now these three remain: faith, hope and love. But the greatest of these is love. 1 Corinthians 13:13 NIV

Chapter 1

"Now that you're all here. I have an announcement."

Jo braced herself for what was coming next. Delta, her close friend and cook/baker, was only a couple weeks away from her wedding, and each passing day brought a new crisis.

"Here we go again." Laverne groaned. "Let me guess...instead of sparklers for your sendoff, you want bottle rockets."

"Don't be ridiculous. Bottle rockets are dangerous." Delta shot her an annoyed look. "I've finally found the perfect dress."

1

Delta was obsessed with every detail of her upcoming nuptials, and she'd struggled with picking out her wedding dress.

Jo chalked it up to her being nervous about the number of people she and Gary had invited. Many of Divine's residents were on the guest list, and even she was beginning to wonder if there would be enough room at the farm for everyone.

Laverne, Jo's newest resident, tapped her foot impatiently. "Let's get this show on the road. Show us what you've got."

"The dress is on my bed. I'll be right back." Delta darted out of the living room.

While Jo and the residents threw out guesses about what Delta's dress would look like, none of them were prepared for what she was wearing when she waltzed back into the room. "Well?"

Jo said the first thing that popped into her head. "You're kidding."

Laverne sputtered and then burst out laughing. "What in the world?"

Delta shoved a hand on her hip. "What do you mean...what in the world?"

"I...I know you're adamant about not wanting a fancy wedding, but I'm not sure this is the right dress." Jo sprang from the chair and circled her camo-clad friend. Upon closer inspection, the camo-pattern wasn't the worst part; that was the color of the inside trim and matching ruffles that encircled the neckline and then flowed all the way to the hemline.

"You look..." Jo struggled to describe the dress without hurting her friend's feelings.

"She looks like she's headed to a pumpkin patch," Laverne shrieked. "Gary's gonna take one look at that getup and run."

"Laverne," Jo chided. "It's not...quite that bad."

Delta plucked at the crinkly jack-o-lantern colored material. "I thought it would fit right in with the country theme."

"It would be a perfect fit if you were getting married on Halloween under a full moon." Laverne howled.

"Laverne." Jo held up a hand. "That's enough."

"I think it's nice," Leah said kindly.

"Yeah." Kelli nodded. "It fits you well, showing just enough cleavage but not too much."

"That's the look I was going for." Delta turned to Jo. "You really don't like it?"

"I like it but perhaps not for a wedding dress," Jo said gently.

Delta flopped down in the chair and propped her cowboy boots on the ottoman as she leaned her head back and closed her eyes. "Finding a dress is going to be the death of me."

"No, it's not. Let me make a quick call." Jo made a beeline for her office and called the first person who came to mind.

"Claire's Collectibles and Antiques, Claire speaking."

"Hey, Claire. It's Jo. I need help." She briefly filled her in on Delta's dress dilemma and asked her if she knew of a local dress shop that sold off-the-rack special occasion dresses. "She doesn't want to wear white. I think something in champagne or silver would look very nice."

"Poor Delta," Claire sympathized. "She was in here the other day looking for wedding accessories. I thought she had a dress picked out."

"It's camo," Jo said bluntly.

There was a moment of silence. "As in – hunting camo?"

"Yep."

5

Claire chuckled. "I guess camo would be fitting for Delta."

"But not for a wedding."

"There's a little shop halfway between here and Smithville." Claire rattled off the shop's information and wished her luck before hanging up.

Delta was still slumped in the chair when Jo returned. "Claire gave me the name of a small shop not far from here. We'll head over there tomorrow. If you all want to tag along, I'm sure Gary and Nash can hold down the fort and handle the bakeshop and mercantile for a couple hours."

"I think it sounds like fun," Michelle said.

"I'm in." Raylene extended a hand and helped Delta from the chair. "Your dress screams Delta all day long, but Jo is right. I think you should look for something more subtle."

"Me too," Kelli agreed.

With a plan in place for the following day, the women each went their separate ways to begin their morning shifts.

It was Raylene's turn to help Delta. She followed Jo into the kitchen while Delta headed to her room to swap out her camo dress for work clothes. She joined them moments later, her expression glum. "I was so sure I had found the perfect dress."

"The camo is very Delta-ish, just not for your wedding."

"Raylene is right," Jo agreed. "We'll find you a perfect dress. When we do, you'll love it."

While Delta and Raylene began working on treats for the baked goods shop, Jo made her way to her office to catch up on some paperwork.

Laverne had recently completed her probationary period, but not without navigating through a few rough patches, mainly because Delta and Laverne, who, like Delta, had been a former prison cook, butted heads.

Thankfully, Laverne had finally accepted the fact that even though Delta was getting married and moving in with Gary, she wasn't planning on hanging up her apron and retiring.

Instead, Laverne had decided to rule the roost at the women's quarters, something the other residents either didn't notice or didn't care about. Jo suspected it was probably a little of both.

After catching up on her paperwork, she checked her emails. Pastor Murphy had promised to help Jo fill her vacancy at the farm. With the exception of a couple troublemakers and one resident who ran off, the pastor had been instrumental in helping place women who needed a fresh start after being released from prison.

There was a light rap, and Jo looked up to find Laverne standing in the doorway. "Hello, Laverne."

"I'm sorry to bother you. I wondered if you had a minute to chat."

"Of course." Jo motioned her inside. "Is everything all right?"

"Yeah. I mean, I'm fine." Laverne shot a tentative glance at the empty hallway behind her. "It's kind of a sensitive topic."

"I see. Please close the door behind you and have a seat." Jo waited for the woman to ease the door shut. "What's on your mind?"

"I'm concerned about Delta," she blurted out.

"You're concerned about Delta," Jo repeated.

"I think she's suffering from a severe case of gamophobia."

"Gamo-what?"

"Gamophobia. The fear of getting married."

Jo leaned back in her chair. "Delta's never been married before. It's perfectly natural for her to be a little stressed out. Are you saying this because of the camo dress?"

"That, and because of some other minor incidents."

"Such as," Jo prompted.

"The wedding cake."

"Has Delta said something about not wanting you to make the wedding cake?" If that were the case, she would be surprised. In fact, Delta seemed relieved to hand off the task to someone else.

"I've come up with half a dozen fabulous cake ideas, but she's shot down every single one. I'm running out of time, and I don't want to be blamed for the cake not being ready."

"I appreciate you letting me know. I'll talk to Delta," Jo promised.

"Thanks." Laverne slid out of the chair and hesitated when she reached the door.

"Is there something else?"

"Maybe."

"What is it?"

"I…" Laverne shifted her feet, looking uncomfortable.

"Is it about Delta?"

"No. It's about you."

"What about me?"

"You exhibit some passive tendencies. I was wondering if you're having trouble handling headstrong Delta."

"You've mentioned that before." Jo tilted her head. "Are you trying to psychoanalyze me?"

"I don't mean to. It's a bad habit."

"Mental issues are best left to the professionals. Besides, I'm not passive; at least I don't think I am."

"I studied clinical mental health at a community college back in the day."

"Great," Jo joked. "All we need is you attempting to treat us for mental issues."

"I'm only trying to help. Sometimes it's easier for an outsider to notice things. I probably shouldn't have said anything, although I am a little worried about the cake."

After Laverne left, Jo stared at the door for a long time. Was she passive? Jo didn't think so. Yes, Delta had her share of days when she was more like a bulldozer than a wallflower. She was headstrong and opinionated, but she was a loyal friend as well.

Jo dismissed the seeds of doubt Laverne had planted and wandered into the kitchen.

Raylene stood in front of the oven, easing muffin tins onto the racks while Delta loaded the dishwasher.

"Whatever you're baking is making me hungry." Jo sniffed appreciatively.

"We finished making my cinnamon apple cakes. They've been flying off the bakery shelves ever since we started offering samples. I set one aside for dessert tonight."

"I can't wait to try it." Jo leaned her hip against the counter, watching her friend. "I finished my office work and wondered if now might be a good time to head over to Gary's to take a look at your fabric samples."

"Yes, ma'am. I've been itching to get a second opinion." Delta wiped her hands on the towel as she motioned to Raylene. "You gonna be okay here by yourself?"

"Got it covered." Raylene gave them a thumbs up.

As soon as Duke, Jo's hound dog, saw her grab the SUV keys, he scrambled out of his doggie bed and met them at the door. "Yes, you can go too."

*****

It was a short drive to Gary's place. The farmhouse was similar to others in the area. It was in need of a fresh coat of paint, and the slightly sagging front porch could use some shoring up.

As soon as Delta opened her door, Duke scrambled across her lap, making a hasty exit. "Duke's already going after those pesky roosters."

"I didn't know Gary had roosters."

"He doesn't. They belong to the neighbor down the road."

Jo paused when she reached the bottom step. "C'mon, Duke." She herded her dog into the house and then followed Delta to the main bedroom in the back. The faded blue wallpaper reminded Jo of her grandmother's from decades ago.

The blue shag carpet was threadbare in spots, creating a visible path from the door all the way around Gary's antique four-poster bed.

Delta caught her staring at it. "The carpet is awful, but there are beautiful hardwood floors underneath. Gary promised we can take this old carpet up and have the floors refinished."

"That would help...update things."

"It's gonna need a lot more than refinishing floors, but I'm up to the challenge. In fact, I'm excited about it." Delta reached for a pile of fabric sitting on the corner chair. "This is what I have so far."

The women sifted through the different patterns and material before narrowing it down to two. "I'll let Gary pick from these. That way, he'll have a say."

"I think that's a great idea." Jo consulted her watch. "We should head back home. C'mon, Duke."

Duke, who had been exploring inside, trotted onto the porch, his ears perking up when he spotted a cluster of chickens pecking the ground nearby.

Delta shook her head. "Gary's tried everything to get rid of them. I should bring them home for Leah."

"Speaking of chickens, Carrie Ford called last night. She's coming by with Leah's chickens today or tomorrow."

Delta waved her hands. "Go on and get out of here before I make fried chicken out of you." The birds began squawking and flapping their wings as they scurried just out of reach.

"Go get 'em, Duke." That was all the encouragement that the hound needed. He barked excitedly and began chasing them around the yard. One of them managed to sneak up behind him and let out a loud *cluck*.

Duke turned tail and began chasing after it. They zigzagged through the front yard before rounding the side of the barn and disappearing from sight.

Jo ran after him. "Duke!" It was too late. The dog was long gone. "Looks like we're going to have to go after him." Jo tossed her purse onto the driver's seat, and she and Delta followed the pup's path around the side of the barn.

When they got there, the chickens were gone, and Duke was circling an old well.

Woof. Duke barked excitedly.

Jo waded through the tall grass.

Duke lowered onto his haunches and barked again.

"Stubborn hound." Jo reached for Duke's collar and then noticed something sticking out from beneath the wooden cover surrounding the handpump.

Her eyes grew wide when it dawned on her what Duke was barking at. "Hey, Delta! I think you need to see this."

Chapter 2

Delta fought her way through the tall grass. "What is it?"

"This." Jo kept a tight grip on Duke's collar as she motioned to the well's cover.

Delta crept forward and sucked in a sharp breath. "It looks like human bones sticking out."

"I was thinking the same thing. We need something to pry the lid off." Jo surveyed their surroundings and spied a stack of metal next to the barn. "What's over there?"

"Gary tore down an old storage shed last year and hasn't gotten around to hauling it to the salvage yard yet. I'll see if I can find something to help us move the cover." Delta jogged over to the pile. She sifted through the pieces and returned carrying a foot-long rod.

Jo coaxed her pup back and watched as her friend eased the rod's flat end under the corner of the cover before prying it up. The weathered slab of wood split in two as clumps of dirt and debris tumbled to the ground.

With the cover off, small bones were now clearly visible. "I think it's time to call the sheriff's department."

"You do that, and I'll call Gary." Delta carefully returned the lid to its original position. "We left our phones in the SUV."

The women trekked back around to the front and stood several yards apart as they placed the calls, both finishing at the same time.

"Gary is on his way," Delta said after joining her friend.

"So are the police." Jo shaded her eyes and stared in the direction of the disturbing discovery. "I hate to say it, but something tells me there's more than just a hand back there."

"I was thinking the same thing."

Since Gary was only a stone's throw away, he arrived first. Delta escorted him to the spot while Jo waited for the authorities. Within minutes, Smith County Sheriff Bill Franklin pulled into the driveway.

His expression was grim as he exited his car. "Morning, Jo."

"Good morning, Sheriff Franklin."

"Heard you found something of interest here on Gary's property."

"Actually, Duke found it." As they walked, Jo told him how they'd been picking out fabrics inside the house. "After finishing, we were on our way to my vehicle when Duke started chasing the neighbor's chickens. We went after him and found him out back, near an old well."

They rounded the corner. Delta and Gary stood staring at the hand pump, talking in low voices. The couple grew silent as the sheriff and Jo approached. "Hello, Bill."

"Gary, Delta." The sheriff tipped his hat before turning his attention to the human remains. "Looks like someone moved the cover."

The women exchanged a quick glance. "We weren't sure what it was at first, so we used a piece of metal to move it aside," Jo explained.

The sheriff slowly circled the pump. "I'll need to call in our crime scene unit." He motioned to Gary. "You have any idea what this might be?"

"No. I haven't been back here since last summer when I tore my shed down. I stacked the pieces behind the barn but paid no mind to anything else. This well hasn't worked since the sixties."

"I'll be right back. I'm sure I don't have to tell you not to touch anything." The sheriff excused himself to place a call.

Delta waited until he was gone. "What if there's a body buried here?"

Gary sucked in a breath. "If there is, it's news to me."

The sheriff was gone for a long time, and Jo was beginning to wonder if perhaps he had left. "I'll see what's keeping Sheriff Franklin." She turned to go and stopped short when he, along with a small army of men carrying boxes, trudged across the field and joined them.

With brief introductions, the men split up. One began securing the area with crime scene tape while two more spread out and began combing the surrounding area. The final two carefully removed the well's wooden cover.

Gary and the women hovered off to the side, watching them work. It was a slow process as they moved a small amount of dirt, sifted through it, took photos and then moved on to another section.

Jo's eyes were drawn to the hand, wondering who it belonged to and why it was there. The excavating abruptly stopped. One of the workers removed a bristle brush from his box and began brushing the dirt. Curious to find out what they'd uncovered, she crept closer.

Her breath caught in her throat as more human remains became visible, along with strips of rubber banding, something that might be used on the inside of a pair of slacks or underwear.

The man traded the brush for a small pick. Using the sharp end, he tapped the ground. While he worked, he said something to the other investigator. Unfortunately, Jo was too far away to hear what he'd said.

He set the pick aside before gently prying a round disc from the earth. He rubbed his thumb across the surface and then held it up. It glinted in the bright sunlight as he turned it over. He placed the object in a plastic baggie before setting it next to the human remains.

Sheriff Franklin, who had left the area before the discovery, returned. The investigator handed the baggie to him.

Franklin studied the contents and carried it over to the trio. "Do you recognize this?"

Gary squinted his eyes. "No, but I can't see too much of it."

"It appears to be a pocket watch." The sheriff returned the piece to the investigators, who were moving at a snail's pace.

Jo glanced at her phone. "I have to get going. There's a call I need to take."

"I think I'm gonna hang out here with Gary," Delta said.

"Take your time." Jo patted the man's arm. "Same for you, Gary."

Gary nodded absentmindedly, his eyes never leaving the scene.

During the drive, Jo prayed for whoever was found by the well. She was far from an expert on gravesites and bodies, but it appeared the remains had been there for some time.

Back at the farm, Nash flagged her down as soon as she exited her vehicle. "What's going on? Gary tore out of here saying something about bones."

"Duke chased the neighbor's chickens out behind Gary's barn. Delta and I went after him. When we got there, we found him standing next to an old well. As I got closer, I thought it looked like there was a human hand sticking out of it." Jo briefly told him what had happened. "The investigators are excavating the site. I think there's a good chance they'll find an entire body back there."

"No kidding."

"It looks as if the bones have been there for some time." Jo shifted her feet. "Can you recall anyone going missing within the last couple of years?"

Nash rubbed the stubble on his chin. "Now that you mention it, there was a guy, a drifter, a year or so back who got in trouble with some area business owners. One day, he was here and the next, he was gone."

"Was it a young guy? An old guy? Do you remember his name?"

"Not off the top of my head."

"I guess we'll have to wait to see what the investigators come up with." Jo returned to the house and found Raylene in the kitchen working on lunch.

"I was wondering what happened to you." Raylene watched Jo wash her hands and grab an apron off the hook. "You left Delta at Gary's place?"

"I did. The investigators are digging up bones out behind Gary's barn."

"Bones?" Raylene's jaw dropped. "As in human remains?"

"I believe so. Duke was out chasing chickens. He's the one who found them. I contacted the police. Sheriff Franklin showed up and came to the same conclusion. He called the investigators in, and they're excavating the site now."

"Does Gary have any idea who it might be?"

"Not yet, and it's a little premature to speculate exactly what happened, so it's probably best to keep this to ourselves."

Raylene made a zipping motion across her lips. "My lips are sealed."

The back porch door flew open, and Laverne appeared. "Is Delta or Gary around? I came up with another cake idea."

"They're not."

"Are they coming back soon?"

"I hope so."

Laverne waved the papers she was holding in the air. "They sure do get a lot of time to goof off. I wish the rest of us had that kind of freedom."

"Goof off?" Jo's eyes narrowed.

"You know. Gallivanting around the countryside with nary a care in the world. All the while, we're stuck here working our tails off."

"First of all, Gary gets paid very little to help with the gardens. Delta is on call almost twenty-four/seven, not to mention she's trying to plan her wedding," Jo pointed out.

Laverne lifted her hands. "I know they're your friends, and it's only right for you to defend them. I just thought I would point out that some of us notice things like who's pulling their weight around here. I'll try to get with Gary later."

Jo clenched her jaw, refusing to take the bait as she watched Laverne hustle out of the kitchen. Seconds later, the door slammed.

"She's a trip." Raylene chuckled.

"More like split, as in split personality. One minute, she can't do enough to help someone, and the next, she's complaining about them. Has she mentioned that she studied psychiatry at one time?"

"Seriously? Well, that explains a lot. She's always trying to analyze me. To hear her talk, I'm never going to find a man because I'm apathetic."

Jo lifted a brow. "Apathetic?"

"I won't let her get under my skin. It drives her nuts."

Jo's watch chimed. "That's my phone call reminder." She hurried to the back, making it in time to take a call from Kelli's probation officer. The women had a productive conversation with Jo reassuring her that her resident was doing well and that Jo had no concerns.

The call ended, and Jo jotted a few notes in Kelli's file, making it back to the kitchen in time to help set the table for lunch.

During the meal, one of the residents commented about Delta and Gary's absence. Jo made an excuse and quickly changed the subject.

Nash hung back after lunch ended, waiting for the residents to leave. "I think I may have found something about Duke's discovery."

"Can you show it to me?" Jo led Nash to her office. She turned her computer on and then shifted to the side, watching as he opened a new search screen. He typed *Barnaby Iteen, Divine, Kansas.*

Several results popped up. Nash clicked on the one at the top. A picture of a man, in his thirties, if Jo had to guess, with a scraggly beard and long unkempt dark hair popped up.

Nash leaned back, waiting while Jo read the brief article below the photo. Written the previous year, it was about a man named Barnaby Iteen who had gotten into trouble with the local authorities, mostly for minor stuff...petty theft, drug possession, breaking and entering.

After finishing, she read a second article and then a third. "So, what happened to the man?"

"Like I said, one day, he just disappeared. Whether this is the person who Duke found behind Gary's place, who knows."

There was a muffled knock on the door, and Delta stuck her head around the corner. "Oh. I thought you were alone."

Jo motioned her inside. "C'mon in. We've been wondering what happened."

"It's a mess." Delta didn't wait for an invitation as she sank down in a chair. "Your hunch was right. There was somebody buried right next to the old pump. From what Gary and I can figure out, all the authorities have to go on is a pocket watch and what's left of the person's clothing."

"Is Gary all right? I can only imagine how disturbing our discovery is for him."

"He's home." Delta placed her hand on her forehead and closed her eyes. "I've been doing some thinking."

Chapter 3

From the look on Delta's face, Jo knew whatever she was going to say wasn't going to be good.

"I'm thinking about postponing the wedding."

Jo placed a light hand on the back of the chair. "Delta, the wedding is only a couple weeks away."

"Surely, you don't think Gary killed someone." Nash folded his arms. "I've known Gary for years. He's no killer."

Delta shifted uncomfortably. "I don't think he has anything to do with that man's body, even though it was on his property."

"Have you talked to Gary?" Jo quietly asked.

"Not yet. I didn't have the heart to add to Gary's anxiety. Besides, I don't want to make a knee-jerk reaction and plan to sleep on it before making a final decision."

"Jo and I were talking...do you remember Barnaby Iteen?"

"The name rings a bell. Wasn't he the creepy guy who showed up in town one day looking for odd jobs and causing problems wherever he went?"

Nash and Delta discussed several of Barnaby's past offenses. Delta's recollections were similar to what Nash remembered, mentioning his petty theft and a run-in with the law regarding drugs.

"I gotta go." Delta scooched out of her chair. "My niece drove by Gary's place earlier and noticed the cop cars. She left a message wanting to know what was going on."

Jo hadn't given a thought to how many Divine locals may have driven by his place and noticed the same thing. She suspected there was a good chance the news had already spread through the small town of Divine like wildfire.

Nash left not long after Delta, but not before reminding Jo about their nightly evening date on the porch swing.

Jo wandered to the window, staring out as she silently prayed for whoever had been buried in the shallow grave. She also prayed for Gary and Delta and that Delta wouldn't make the wrong decision.

She thought about her friend, Marlee. If anyone knew to what extent the news had spread, it would be the owner of Divine Delicatessen.

Marlee wasted no time confirming Jo's suspicions. "Hey, Jo. What's going on over at Gary's place?"

"Delta and I went by there this morning to look at some fabric. Duke was with us. He started chasing the neighbor's chickens and led us to what appears to be a shallow grave."

"No kidding. Do you have any idea who it was?"

"Not yet. Whoever it was has been there for a while. We're still waiting to find out."

"I'm sure Delta and Gary are beside themselves," Marlee said. "She's already in a tizzy about this wedding. I can only imagine what's going through Delta's mind – not to mention Gary's – right now. I hate to say it, but she's been giving me a few warning signs that she might be getting cold feet."

"I've gotten the same feeling," Jo admitted.

"Do you think she'll back out?"

"I don't know. Delta's understandably upset."

"If that happens, the tongues are going to wag," Marlee predicted. "Gary and Delta's wedding is the talk of the town. Throw in a dead body, and we'll probably have a slew of reporters crawling all over the place."

Jo hadn't considered what might happen if the local news picked up the story. "I hope not."

"I'll keep my ear to the ground." There was a voice in the background, and Marlee became distracted. "Look, I have to go. Tell Delta to hang in there."

Jo promised she would and then wandered into the kitchen, where she found Delta seated at the table, a plate of leftovers in front of her.

"Care for some company?"

"Sure. Misery loves company."

Jo eased into the empty chair and watched as her friend picked at the food. "I'm all ears if you want to talk."

Delta sucked in a breath. "I called Gary after I talked to my niece. Most of the town already knows what happened. He said his property is covered in so much yellow tape, you can hardly walk around."

"Did they find more than one body?"

"No. It was only one set of skeletal remains...one too many." Delta sawed off a small piece of lasagna. "I don't know what to do."

"About the wedding," Jo guessed.

"If I postpone it, people are going to say I think Gary is responsible."

"Do you think there's a chance he knows more than he's letting on?"

Delta paused as she considered Jo's question. "I hope not. I mean, I don't think so. Shoot. I'm so confused right now."

"We'll know more as soon as the investigators can identify the remains." Jo brushed an imaginary crumb off the table. "In the meantime, if you haven't changed your mind by tomorrow morning, I think we should keep our plans. We'll go dress shopping and then out to lunch."

"I guess it can't hurt." Delta's chair made a loud scraping sound as she shoved it back. "I think I'm gonna turn in early."

"I'll see you in the morning." Jo gave her a quick hug. "It'll be all right. You'll see." She waited for Delta's bedroom door to close before making her way into the living room.

She flipped through the television channels, but nothing caught her interest. Giving up, she turned the television off and tossed the remote on the sofa before stepping out onto the porch for some fresh air.

She eased onto the porch swing while Duke sprawled out on the floor next to her.

Twinkling stars lit up the night sky as crickets played a merry tune. The occasional croak of a bullfrog joined in. She nudged the swing with the tip of her shoe, gazing up at the starry sky.

A lone figure coming from the direction of the women's housing units appeared from the shadows. Moving at a fast clip, Raylene passed under the mercury light.

Jo gave a quick wave to catch her attention. Picking up the pace, Raylene hustled across the yard, stopping when she reached the porch's bottom step. "Mind if I join you?"

"Of course not." Jo patted the empty spot on the swing.

Raylene greeted Duke with a pat on the head before plopping down next to her. "I saw Gary drop Delta off a little while ago. How're they doing?"

"I'm not sure about Gary, but Delta is freaking out. She mentioned postponing the wedding." Jo nudged the floor again, and they began to swing. "She's sleeping on it."

"If she does decide to postpone the wedding, people will think she suspects Gary."

"It won't look good."

"Guilt before innocence." Raylene grew quiet for a moment. "I guess that means we're not going dress shopping tomorrow."

"We're still going. After we're done, I'm treating everyone to lunch. There's a new restaurant over in Smithville I've been itching to try."

"Which will depend on whether or not Gary shows up for work tomorrow. If not, we won't have anyone to help Nash run the mercantile and bakeshop."

"True," Jo murmured. "I guess we'll have to play it by ear and wait until tomorrow morning to see what happens."

Raylene started to say something but stopped.

Jo waited. "Is there something else on your mind?"

"There is." Raylene reached into her pocket. She pulled out an envelope and handed it to Jo. "I got this in the mail today."

Jo held it up, using the soft glow of the living room window lamp to see. Handwritten in neat letters on the envelope's front was Raylene's name along with the farm's address. She flipped it over, searching for a return address. "Aaron Beck, Sarasota, FL. What is this?"

"It's a letter from Brock's younger brother, Aaron. It's self-explanatory." Raylene sprang from the swing and switched the porch light on while Jo removed the single sheet of paper.

Dear Raylene,

I hired one of Brock's bounty hunter buddies to track you down after discovering you'd been released from Central State Women's Penitentiary. This Divine, Kansas address is listed as your last known address. I hope you don't mind.

If you receive this letter, please call me at...

The brief letter listed a cell phone number and was signed, *Cordially, Aaron Beck.*

Jo read it a second time before placing it back inside the envelope. "Are you going to call him?"

"At first, I was dead set against it, but...maybe it's time for some closure." Raylene's hand shook as she took the envelope. "Aaron said some terrible things about me during my trial."

"It can't hurt to see what he has to say," Jo said quietly.

"That's what I was thinking."

"Maybe you should do what Delta is and sleep on it. If you decide to call him, you can stop by my office and use my cell phone." One of Jo's house rules was no resident was allowed a personal cell phone, and any calls made needed to be approved by Jo or Delta.

"Maybe I'll wait until after we come back from the shopping trip."

"Whenever you're ready."

"Thanks, Jo." Raylene switched the porch light off. "I better get going. I'm sure Nash will be along shortly to keep you company. I'll see you in the morning."

"See you in the morning." After Raylene left, Jo resumed her swinging, deep in thought. She wondered how Gary was doing. How *had* skeletal remains ended up on his property? Would Delta back out of the wedding at this late date?

She thought about the note Raylene received. What did Brock's brother want after all of these years? Since he went through all of the trouble and expense of hiring someone to track her down, it must be important to him.

"Hey."

Startled, Jo jumped, clutching her chest.

Nash climbed the steps. "Sorry, I thought you saw me coming."

"No, I didn't."

He greeted Duke and then leaned in for a kiss. "How's that for a greeting?"

"Much better than you scaring me half to death. It makes my heart race in a different way," she flirted.

"Then I accomplished my goal." He eased in next to her and reached for her hand. "How's Delta?"

"She's okay. I'm not so sure about Gary, though."

"I talked to him. He's rattled. He said his property looks like a major crime scene."

"Delta made a similar comment."

"Do you think she'll call the wedding off?"

"I don't know," Jo said. "I have to confess, I'm not sure what I would do if I were in her shoes. I mean, we found him...her...whoever it was on his property."

They discussed the possibilities, and then the conversation drifted to the following day's schedule. "Gary assured me he'll be here in the morning so you can take Delta dress shopping."

"I appreciate that." Jo snuggled closer, feeling his warmth through his cotton shirt. The stars twinkled brightly in the clear night air, and the couple began making a game out of naming the constellations.

"I give up. It's apparent I need to brush up on my star gazing." A light breeze blew, and Jo involuntarily shivered.

"Uh-oh. You're getting cold. I guess it's time to end our porch date," Nash teased.

"Not yet. Stay here. I have a treat for us." Jo dashed inside and hurried to the kitchen. It took a few minutes of rummaging around in the pantry until she found the container of hot chocolate.

She quickly whipped up two cups and then sprinkled some mini-marshmallows on top. On her way out, she tossed the couch's throw over her shoulder.

Nash held the door, cautiously taking one of the steaming mugs from her as she stepped onto the porch. "Hot chocolate. This is a treat."

He waited for Jo to settle in on the swing before tucking the throw around her.

"Thank you. I know this isn't a summer drink, but it sounded good."

"It's delicious." Nash lifted his mug. "Here's to snuggling under the stars."

Jo tapped her mug to his. "To snuggling under the stars." The hot chocolatey goodness warmed her all the way down to the tips of her toes.

They talked about the farm, the gardens and the women's progress, comparing notes. "Have you figured out when you plan to fill the vacancy?"

"I've been putting it off until after the wedding...if there is a wedding." Jo cradled the mug. "No sense in adding more stress."

"I agree."

A yawn escaped, and Jo covered her mouth. "Excuse me."

"It's getting late." Nash reluctantly stood. "Something tells me tomorrow is going to be one of those days."

"Unfortunately, I think you may be right." She reached for Nash's mug, but he refused to let go. Instead, he seized the opportunity to pull Jo to him. He slipped an arm around her waist as he lowered his lips. The kiss was sweet and tender, leaving her breathless when he finally pulled away. "I love you, Jo."

"I love you too, Nash," she whispered. "I love our porch swing date evenings."

"Me too."

Her smile lingered as she watched him amble down the steps. When he reached the stairs leading to his apartment, he turned back, giving Jo a wave before disappearing from sight.

"C'mon, Duke. It's time for bed." She coaxed the pup inside, locking the door behind them. She tossed the throw on the couch on the way to the kitchen, where she made quick work of washing the mugs.

Jo left the light above the sink on and checked the back door. Passing by the small hall that led to Delta's bedroom and bath, she caught a glimmer of light beneath the door.

She thought about knocking and then decided against it. Instead, she whispered a prayer for her friends.

Despite the day's events, Jo slept through the night and woke early the next morning.

The first order of business was to let Duke out. Hungry, the pup wasted no time taking care of business before trotting back inside.

The tantalizing aroma of fresh coffee wafted all the way into the dining room. She stepped inside the kitchen and found Delta seated at the table. A yellow pad of paper was in front of her. "Good morning."

"Morning, Jo."

Jo filled an empty cup and took a seat next to her friend. She cast a glance at the yellow pad and then did a double-take when she caught the heading at the top. "Delta, what is this?"

Chapter 4

"It's me trying to figure out if I should marry Gary. You know, where you make a list. On one side are the why's. On the other side are the why not's." Delta slid the pad of paper across the table. "Here's what I've come up with."

Jo reached for her reading glasses. "Reasons to call it off. Marrying might mess up a good thing. Losing my independence. The drive to work."

She began reading the second column. "Reasons to marry Gary. I love him. I won't find anyone who loves me like he does. A lot of planning has gone into the wedding. I can check it off my bucket list."

Jo silently re-read the list.

"Well?"

"You put driving to work as a con? Yeah, your commute is gonna be brutal," Jo teased.

"Granted, it's only a coupla minutes down the road, but it's still getting out of the house, getting in the truck and making the drive." Delta walked her index and middle finger across the table. "Right now, all I gotta do is walk from my bedroom to the kitchen. It's twenty steps, tops."

"I can check it off my bucket list." Jo wrinkled her nose. "Getting married is on your bucket list?"

"Sure. I mean, I didn't figure it would ever happen, but I hoped one day it would."

"Getting married isn't on my bucket list. As a matter of fact, I don't have one."

"You don't have a bucket list?" Delta's eyes widened in horror. "I thought everyone over fifty had one."

"I'm barely fifty," Jo joked. "Maybe I'll start one next year." She took a sip of coffee and eyed her friend over the rim of the cup. "What else is on your bucket list besides getting married?"

"I have a few things," Delta mumbled.

Jo's curiosity was piqued. "Like what?"

"I suppose..." Delta rolled her eyes. "I would like to be our festival's parade marshal. I want to visit the Grand Canyon, create my own cookbook, learn Siouan."

"What's Siouan?"

"The Kansas Creek Reservation's language." Delta perked up. "It's a lost art. Chief Tallgrass and his tribe are the last people known to be fluent in the language. Kansa, a Siouan tribe, named Kansas which meant 'people of the south wind.'"

"You could ask them to teach it to you. At least it wouldn't hurt to ask. I'm sure you could pull some strings and get a spot on a parade float." Jo twirled her cup in a slow circle. "As far as the cookbook, we can do a little research to find out how to make that happen. Perhaps you and Gary should visit the Grand Canyon on a belated honeymoon."

"You're talking about a looong drive," Delta drawled. "We'd end up killing each other being cooped up in a car for that many hours. I would be just as happy spending the weekend scooter-pooting around to flea markets and whatnot."

"Whatever you decide, we'll hold down the fort." Jo refilled both of their cups before resuming her place at the table. "Are you going to postpone the wedding?"

"I'm on the fence. I think it would break Gary's heart."

"Getting married is a life-changing decision, something one should never take lightly," Jo said gently. "In the meantime, the residents are looking forward to dress shopping and lunch today."

"You sure I can't..."

Jo cut her off. "I'm sorry, but the camo dress you picked out will not work."

"I kinda figured it was a little out there." Delta sighed heavily. "I'm not one for shopping."

"It will be fun." Jo downed the last of her coffee and patted her friend's hand as she shoved her chair back. "I promise."

While Delta began working on breakfast, Jo showered and made her way to her office to catch up on some bookwork. Marlee checked in to find out if Jo had an update. "Nothing yet. We're going dress shopping and out to lunch."

"So, the wedding is still on."

"As far as I know. What's the gossip around town?"

"Carrie Ford was in here first thing this morning. She said she thinks it might be Barnaby Iteen."

Jo remembered her conversation with Nash the evening before. "Nash mentioned his name too. He said he was a drifter who worked odd jobs."

"And trouble with a capital 'T.' He spent a lot of time hanging out at the Half Wall Bar, which is where he picked up some of his jobs, at least that's what I heard."

When pressed, Marlee didn't know why Carrie thought the remains belonged to Iteen. Knowing Carrie, it wouldn't be long before she showed up on Jo's doorstep to snoop and try to get the scoop.

The friends chatted for a few more minutes before there was a tentative knock on the door. Raylene appeared. Noticing Jo was on the phone, she started to back away. Jo waved her inside. "Hey, Marlee. I need to get going."

Jo told her good-bye and set her cell phone on the desk. "Good morning, Raylene."

"Morning." Raylene timidly tucked a stray strand of hair behind her ear as she hovered in the doorway. "I was wondering if I could place the call to Aaron Beck so I can get it over with."

"Yes. Yes, of course." Jo began making her way around the desk. "I forgot all about it."

"Thanks. I...it shouldn't take long."

"Take your time." Jo started to leave.

"Wait." Raylene stopped her. "Do you mind hanging around while I make the call? Depending on what he says, I might need a little moral support."

"Sure." Jo offered her an encouraging smile, noting the dark circles under her resident's eyes. "You've been worrying about it."

"All night." Raylene nervously rubbed the palms of her hands on her slacks. "I barely slept, wondering what Brock's brother could possibly want with me after all of these years."

"There's only one way to find out."

Raylene slowly made her way across the room. She tentatively reached for the phone and then snatched her hand back.

It was painfully clear she was struggling with her decision, and Jo's heart went out to her. When Raylene arrived at the farm almost a year ago, she was defeated, depressed and suicidal.

In fact, her attempted suicide was how she ended up on Jo's radar in the first place. Raylene had served her time at the Central State Penitentiary. Just hours after her release with nowhere to go, no future and carrying unbearable guilt over the death of her partner, she'd jumped off the Divine Bridge. It was nicknamed "the leap of death," and for very good reason. Until Raylene, no one who had gone over the side had survived.

But God had other plans for Raylene Baxter. According to Evan, a local and an eyewitness to her potentially deadly jump, he had raced to the edge of the ravine. As he looked down into the ravine, Evan had spotted two men with her, but by the time he reached the bottom, the men were gone.

Raylene had not only miraculously survived the fall, but she'd also survived with only minor injuries. Locals were convinced Divine's angelic protectors had saved her. Although some had scoffed at Evan's account, Jo was a believer; and had, in fact, experienced an encounter with Divine's heavenly beings of her own.

The angels had appeared to help, protect and warn Jo and the residents several times over the past year. Even Gary and Leah had caught a glimpse of them.

God had brought Raylene a long way toward healing and forgiving herself for Brock's death.

"God hasn't brought you this far just to bring you down," Jo said softly.

A lone tear ran down Raylene's cheek. "This is hard," she whispered.

"I know." Jo crossed the room and wrapped her arms around the woman's shoulders. "It would be easier to ignore the letter and let it go, but if you do..."

"...then I'll always wonder," Raylene finished her sentence. She sucked in a breath and swiped at her eyes. "There's only one way to find out what Aaron wants."

"There is."

"I'm going to do this."

"You *can* do this." Jo gave her a thumbs up.

"I can do this." Raylene paced back and forth, mumbling under her breath. "He can't hurt me any more than I've already hurt myself."

The pacing and one-sided conversation continued for several long moments, and Jo could only imagine what Raylene was going through.

Making the call could open up every wound, the soul-searching, the endless layers of guilt and the lack of forgiveness.

But Jo wisely understood that no matter what Aaron Beck said to Raylene, the call would be another step toward closure and moving forward.

While some of the other residents would choose to ignore the note, refuse to risk the chance of exposing themselves to more hurt, Raylene was different. Her personality dictated that she deal with things head-on instead of ignoring them or sweeping them under the rug.

In other words, Raylene would have no peace until she made the call.

"I...I'm ready." Raylene's hand shook as she removed Aaron's letter from her pocket. She unfolded the single sheet of paper and then picked up Jo's phone. "Maybe he won't answer."

"You can always leave a message."

"Right." Raylene finished entering the number and then held the phone to her ear as Jo began to pray.

Her face turned an ashen white. "Hello. Is this Aaron?"

Chapter 5

The conversation between Raylene and Brock's brother was brief. From what Jo was able to glean during their one-sided conversation, Aaron was confirming Raylene's location.

"You want to meet with me Wednesday – as in this Wednesday?" Raylene shot Jo a terrified look. "I...might have to get back with you."

Jo nodded her head and mouthed the words, "Wednesday is all right."

"I...uh. Yes. Wednesday is okay. I'm sure I can rearrange my work schedule if necessary. We can meet..."

"Here," Jo whispered loudly.

"Yes, we can meet at the place where I work." Raylene rattled off the address. "Nine will be fine. I'll see you then. Good-bye."

Jo watched as she set the phone on the desk and slumped into the chair. Raylene leaned her head back and closed her eyes. "What did I just get myself into?"

"How did he sound?"

Raylene's eyes popped open. "I couldn't get a read on him. There was no emotion one way or the other."

"Did he say why he wants to see you?"

"To discuss Bay Hill Bail Agents, which was Brock's and my former business."

"All of that can be done via email or over the phone," Jo pointed out.

"I was thinking the same thing, which leads me to believe there's some other reason he wants to see me. He's using the business as an excuse," Raylene said. "He's flying here from Florida for more than to just close down a shell of a business."

"Some time ago, you mentioned you had money."

"I do. It's in a Florida bank account."

"How much money do you have, and would Aaron have a claim to it, as in, was his brother's name tied to the account?"

"It's roughly a hundred thousand. I don't see how Aaron would even know about the money. It was in a personal account with no ties to the business." Raylene's brows furrowed as she contemplated Jo's suggestion. "What if he found out about the money, hired a lawyer and filed a wrongful death suit against me?"

"There's only one way to find out."

"I almost wish he had never tracked me down." Raylene groaned.

"But now that he has, we'll deal with it as it comes along." Jo patted her shoulder. "Agreed?"

"Agreed."

"If, or even when, we reach that point, my friend and attorney, Chris Nyles, will help us."

"Thanks, Jo. I don't know what I would do without you."

Jo followed the woman out of her office. "We're still on for shopping and lunch."

"Count me in. I need something to distract me."

"Shopping is therapy," Jo joked. "We could all use a little therapy."

During breakfast, it was decided that while the women were gone, Gary would run the bakeshop, and Nash would handle the mercantile.

The women all pitched in to help clean up and then piled into two vehicles.

Since Jo had called ahead to confirm the shop was open, the owner of Shabby Chic Bridal Boutique, who was awaiting their arrival, greeted them at the door. Jo stepped inside what was hands down the cutest bridal boutique she'd ever laid eyes on.

"C'mon in, gals." The petite redhead held the door, welcoming them inside where a fresh citrus-scent lingered in the air. "I'm Magnolia Champlain. Which one of you is the nearly married, altar bound, bride-to-be?"

"Me." Delta extended her hand. "Delta Childress soon-to-be Stein."

"It's a pleasure to meet you, Delta." Magnolia clasped Delta's hand as she led her into the open parlor. Lining both sides were opaque white, headless mannequins in an array of poses, each sporting a bridal gown.

The others trailed behind as Magnolia, her voice dripping with Southern charm, described the mannequins' gowns in great detail.

They made it as far as the first row of displays before Delta politely dampened the owner's enthusiasm. "You seem like a very nice woman,

Magnolia, and I appreciate how you're trying to put me at ease. I'm sure you're accustomed to dealing with starry-eyed young women who are in search of the perfect Cinderella wedding dress to wear as they sashay down a rose-petaled aisle to wed their Prince Charming. I, on the other hand, as you can see, am no spring chicken. I have already purchased what I think is the perfect camo dress but my friends, here, shot it down."

"A camo dress?" Magnolia's big brown eyes grew round as saucers as she stared at Delta. "Surely, you jest."

"No, honey, I am as serious as a heart attack. I reluctantly agreed to take a look around your shop for something a little less..."

"Gaudy," Laverne interjected.

Delta shot her a death look. "A little more traditional."

Jo covered her mouth to hide her smile. Delta was making every effort to talk calmly to the southern belle. She knew her friend well enough to know that if she thought she could get away with it, Delta would turn right around and walk out of the bridal shop without looking back.

"I think what Delta's trying to say is that she wants something elegant and eye-catching yet geared toward a more mature bride," Jo said diplomatically.

"And it doesn't have to be white," Delta added. "In fact, I would prefer not to wear white."

"Allow me to point out that white is also acceptable for women marrying for a second time," Magnolia said.

"I've never been married before."

"I see. Well, then I may have something more suitable back here." Magnolia motioned for them to follow her to the rear of the shop where several racks of dresses were located.

"This is better." Delta began sifting through the dresses at a rapid rate. "Too pink. Too Victorian. Looks like a lampshade."

Jo and the others joined in to give her a hand. The women split up, each picking a different rack to peruse. It didn't take long to select several sleek, shimmery evening gowns with folds and seams perfect for accentuating Delta's generous curves.

Magnolia ushered Delta into an empty dressing room with half a dozen dresses in hand while the others waited nearby. At one point, Delta's voice ratcheted up a notch, and Jo braced herself, half-expecting her friend to storm out, but it never happened.

Instead, she emerged wearing a lavender three-quarter silk and taffeta dress.

"It's very nice," Michelle said. "I like the color."

"Honey, did you see the bow in the back?" Delta spun around, revealing a large, black bow. "The bow makes my butt look big, and I don't need any help."

"It is a little large. The bow, I mean." Raylene bit her lower lip to hide her smile. "Next?"

Delta hustled to the back. She swapped out the dress in no time flat, reappearing this time in a cream-colored satin lace dress.

Jo gave it a thumbs up. "I like this one better than the last."

"It's itchy." Delta grimaced as she tugged on the top. "I'll have this thing on half an hour tops."

"Your new husband might like that," Magnolia teased.

Delta rolled her eyes, and Jo knew her friend had almost reached the end of her patience with the sugary-sweet woman. "Nope." She flounced to the dressing room and again, in record time, returned.

"Now that dress is spectacular." Jo clasped her hands.

"Like it was made for you." Kelli nodded her approval.

"I like it too," Michelle said. "So far, it's the best of the bunch."

"You're positively glowing," Leah chimed in.

Magnolia eyed it critically. "I think we have a winner."

Laverne was the only one who didn't comment. Delta pointed at her. "You're never short on opinions. What do you think, Laverne?"

"I...it's okay." She shrugged.

"What don't you like about it?" Delta pressed.

"I'm not a dress kinda gal, so I'm probably not the best person to ask."

"Neither am I. I want your honest opinion."

Laverne shifted uncomfortably. "You're pretty, you know, top-heavy. Maybe something a little less fitted."

"I was thinking the same thing." Delta lowered her gaze, critically eyeing her ample bosom. "I want Gary to appreciate all my womanly curves but maybe not quite this much while we're standing at the altar."

"Absolutely. I have a similar dress I think would fit the bill."

Magnolia and Delta stepped back into the dressing room, and when they emerged, Jo knew they had found "the" dress. The top was a silver lace, and the skirt fell below Delta's knees. The straight lines of the matching jacket gave it an elegant look.

"I love it." Jo slowly circled her friend. "How is the fit?"

Delta bent, turned and then lifted her hands over her head. She made a slow pitch, extending her arm.

"What are you doing?" Jo laughed.

"Tossing the bouquet." Delta approached the trio of mirrors and studied the dress from various angles. "It'll do."

"It's perfect," Raylene said.

"Gary will love it," Kelli predicted.

"We'll take it." Jo reached for her purse. "How much for the dress?"

"It's off the rack." Magnolia rattled off what Jo thought was a reasonable price.

"You can't pay for my dress."

"It's part of my wedding gift to you." Jo nodded toward a jewelry counter nearby. "We need some bling to go with it."

Delta picked out a set of costume pearls and was shocked at the price. Despite her objections, Jo insisted on purchasing those as well. "Something old, something new."

"Something borrowed, something blue," Raylene finished.

"We have the new covered." Jo gave Magnolia her credit card. She rang up the purchases and handed her the receipt before carefully wrapping the dress in a garment bag.

Their next stop was the café. When the women arrived, the hostess seated them at a large table in a quiet corner. The conversation centered around the dress shop and all of the different dresses Delta had tried on.

"Are you sure I didn't look frumpy?" Delta frowned.

"You looked far from frumpy. You looked fabulous," Leah said.

"Without a doubt," Raylene added as the others chimed in their agreement.

Jo lifted her half-full glass of ice water. "I propose a toast."

The others lifted their glasses. "Here's to the most beautiful bride in Divine and the wedding of the decade. May it be all smooth sailing from here on out."

"Here. Here." Delta clinked her glass before taking a big sip.

Their food arrived fast and hot, and the meal flew by. After the women finished eating, the others began making their way to the vehicles while Jo settled the bill. She caught up with them out front. "I had so much fun."

"Me too." Raylene beamed. "It was nice to take my mind off my troubles."

"You got troubles?" Delta asked.

"It's a long story."

"I can't wait to hear it." Delta and her group returned to the truck while Jo and the rest of the residents climbed into her SUV for the trip back to the farm.

Delta was long gone by the time Jo pulled onto the road.

She must've put the pedal to the metal because the truck was already empty, and the women were long gone when they arrived home.

Jo parked in her usual spot and headed to the cargo area to grab Delta's dress and necklace. She carried both inside the house before heading back outside. She found Delta, along with Gary and Nash, standing in front of Nash's workshop, a somber expression on each of their faces.

Chapter 6

"Uh-oh." Jo's heart skipped a beat. "What's wrong?"

"Gary heard back from the authorities," Delta said. "They've identified the remains found at his farm."

"It was Barnaby Iteen, a man I hired to help me." Gary went on to explain that Iteen had shown up at his place one day out of the blue, giving him a sob story about being homeless and needing work. "I felt sorry for him, so I hired him to do some odd jobs around my place. When I found out he was stealing from me, I chased him off my property and told him to never set foot on it again."

"He didn't set foot. He put his whole body on it," Delta said. "How were they able to identify him?"

"His clothing, or what was left of it. That and he was missing part of his right pinky. Got it caught in a grinder was what he told me. Of course, I took anything he said with a grain of salt since he was a thief and a troublemaker."

"Have they determined the cause of death?"

"Nope. According to Sheriff Franklin, it might take some time."

"So, they don't suspect you of murdering him," Jo said.

"That's where it gets a little tricky," Gary said. "Remember when the investigators found that pocket watch? It's mine."

Jo stared at Gary in stunned silence, attempting to digest the news. "The pocket watch belongs to you?"

"They cleaned it up since it was covered with dirt, and I realized it was one I thought I lost. It was right around the time Barnaby was working for me." Gary fished his cell phone from his pocket and tapped the screen. He showed the trio a picture of him holding a silver watch with gold trim. Intricate etchings circled the outside. A compass was in the center. "My grandfather's initials, GES, Gary Edward Stein, are on the back."

"Which are also your initials," Jo guessed.

"Yep."

Nash, who had remained silent so far, finally spoke. "So, now what happens?"

"According to Franklin, since they don't know if a crime was committed or if Iteen died from some other cause, nothing happens right now."

"And it may never go any further," Nash said.

"Franklin wasn't very forthcoming on what would happen next."

A car pulled into the drive, and a couple emerged before heading into the bakeshop.

"I had better get back to work. I need to finish installing the chicken coop wire. Carrie is bringing Leah's chickens by this afternoon."

With everything that was going on, Jo had forgotten about the chickens Carrie had promised Leah. The resident's interest in sustainable living and gardening had piqued, and she'd nearly begged Jo to allow her to have chickens, even insisting she would pay for them using her own money.

Since one of Jo's goals was for the residents to develop an interest, a passion, in something they could use after leaving the farm, she was all for it.

"I'll see you later." Gary attempted a half-hearted smile before trudging off.

Jo waited until he was out of earshot. "Poor Gary. Nothing like having a dark cloud hanging over your head while you're trying to get ready for the big day."

"He'll be all right. We all know Gary's not responsible for Barnaby's death. It's only a matter

of time before the authorities figure out who is."
Nash returned to his workshop and Delta and Jo
made their way into the house.

Duke, who had been outside, followed Jo to her
office. The pup settled in his bed near the window
while she began working on the mercantile's
inventory.

Business was booming now that families were
embarking on their summer road trips. The Divine
area was a popular stop for travelers who were
eager to check out the centermost point of the
contiguous United States.

If the uptick continued, both businesses would
beat the previous year's numbers. With that in
mind, Jo was tossing around the idea of giving each
of the women a well-deserved raise.

She made it through the majority of her
paperwork, and then her mind began to wander.
Duke, sensing her restlessness, woke from his nap
and stared out the window. Jo followed his gaze.

The sun was shining, beckoning them outside to enjoy the beautiful day. Deciding a walk to clear the cobwebs was in order, she led Duke out of the house.

He bolted down the steps and began running in circles, urging Jo to pick up the pace. She had almost caught up with him when she heard a sharp whistle. Laverne stood near the entrance to the bakeshop, flagging her down.

"What's up?"

"It's Delta. I was supposed to help her this afternoon. She kicked me out of the kitchen, saying she didn't need me. Is there anything else I can do? I checked with Nash and the others, and they don't need me either."

"What about cleaning up the common area?"

"Already done. I swept, vacuumed, mopped, cleaned the sinks, the showers and the toilets."

"You can tag along with Duke and me. We're on our way to check on the gardens."

"Sure."

Duke trotted ahead. Familiar with Jo's routine, he led them to the smaller of the gardens. He scampered up and down the rows as Jo trailed behind.

Pleased with the progress, they continued toward the back. Laverne slowed, eyeing the fence line with interest. "Is this the place?"

"If you mean does all of this belong to me, the fence is the boundary. The Kansas Creek Indian Reservation's property starts on the other side."

"No, I mean where the sightings have taken place."

"Ah." Jo lifted a brow as it dawned on her what Laverne was asking. "Our angelic encounters. To answer your question – yes – this is the general vicinity of where I've spotted our mysterious visitors."

"And Leah and Gary have seen them too."

"They have."

"What was the story again about the angels who scared off that convict? I know who she was and even heard the story while I was still incarcerated, but I forgot her name. It was big news around the prison when she escaped."

"Karen Griffin. She planned to rob us but got scared off by two large men who were chasing her."

"The angels."

"According to Ms. Griffin, she said some tall men were chasing her."

"She could've been lying," Laverne said.

"Except for the fact that our neighbor also saw a man. He was moving at a fast clip. When he stepped under one of the mercury lights, he disappeared."

Laverne snapped her fingers. "He vanished into thin air."

"Something like that." Jo cast Laverne a glance. "Have you had an encounter with one?"

"Not yet." Laverne started to say something else and then stopped.

"What is it?" Jo prompted.

"I'm itching to find out if they're hanging around here."

"And?"

"I was thinking if I created some sort of crisis, they might come to my aid."

Jo abruptly stopped. "You can't willy-nilly summon angels to rescue you. Besides, God dispatches angels, and He's all-knowing. Don't you think He would know what you're trying to pull?"

"It was just a thought." Laverne grew quiet as she followed Jo around the beehives. "Do you think Delta's going to go through with the wedding?"

"I hope so."

"Better her than me. I'm a one-and-done kinda gal. I tried the marriage thing a long time ago. It wasn't my cup of tea."

Jo couldn't disagree with Laverne. She'd been married once, as well. And as much as she adored Nash, she was content with their relationship.

"What about you and Nash?"

"What about us?"

"Are you two going to tie the knot?"

"No. I don't know."

"Have you been married before?" Laverne asked. "I mean, I don't mean to be nosy."

Jo answered the question with one of her own. "Are you trying to psychoanalyze me?"

"Maybe." Laverne shrugged. "You don't have to answer. I already know you're divorced. I was just making conversation."

"Yes, I was married. It didn't end horribly. It just ended. We were two different people. I don't like to repeat the same mistake twice."

"You're suffering from pistanthrophobia."

"Pistanthrophobia?"

"Fear of trusting others," Laverne explained. "It's often the result of being seriously disappointed by a prior relationship."

"Like I said, our divorce was amicable."

"So, maybe your commitment phobia goes back even further, to your parents."

Jo felt herself begin to shut down at the mention of her parents. Laverne immediately sensed the change. "I...I'm sorry. Sometimes I don't know when to shut up."

"It's all right," Jo said evenly. "You've touched on a topic I don't discuss." Thankfully, they had reached the large garden, and Jo began perusing the bountiful harvest. There was lettuce, along with string beans, snow peas and carrots.

Laverne stood off to the side and began scratching her arms.

Jo shot her a quick look. "Don't tell me you're allergic to fruits and vegetables."

"No. I crave fresh fruits and vegetables. Poison ivy is another story, and believe me, I've seen some around here." Despite Laverne's denial of allergies, she maintained a safe distance while Jo made her way up and down the rows. After finishing, she joined Laverne, and they began making their way to the front.

They rounded the side of the women's housing unit, past the store and the bakeshop. The parking lot was full. A cluster of nuns, clad head to toe in black except for the white under their veils and coifs, stood nearby.

Two of the nuns were carrying large white bakery boxes.

"Hello," Jo greeted the women. "I'm Joanna Pepperdine, the owner of Divine Baked Goods Shop. Were you able to find everything you were looking for?"

"That and so much more." A robust woman with cherry red cheeks beamed. "I'm Sister Margaret Mary. This is our first visit to your fine establishment. We found out about this place from Pastor Murphy, who stopped by last week to visit with Reverend Mother Calabish."

A second one spoke. "We're from the Sisters of Mercy convent in Smithville."

"Which is also the name of the hospital," Jo said.

"Yes." Sister Margaret Mary nodded. "We've heard about your angelic visits from Reverend Mother and decided to stop by to have a look around."

Laverne cleared her throat and mumbled under her breath. "See? I'm not the only one."

"Not to mention the good work you're doing with the women." The younger of the two who had been speaking turned to Laverne. "Are you a resident?"

"Yes, ma'am. I mean, sister. I don't wanna come off as rude, but I would appreciate it if you didn't try to convert me."

"Convert you?" She shot Laverne a puzzled look. "We're not here for conversions. We're here for delicious baked goods, not to mention admittedly, out of curiosity."

Laverne nervously shifted and then quickly excused herself, hurrying off in the direction of Nash's workshop.

Jo made small talk with the nuns and then thanked them for stopping by before they climbed into a van with the Sisters of Mercy name emblazoned on the side.

Wondering what had happened to Laverne, she crossed the parking lot and found her standing next to a red Dodge minivan. Carrie Ford, along with Gary, Leah and Nash, stood on the other side.

"Hello, Carrie."

"Hey, Jo." Carrie slid her sunglasses on top of her head. "I'm delivering Leah's hens."

"She's been anxiously awaiting their arrival."

A loud clucking emanated from the back as Carrie reached inside and removed a metal cage. She handed the cage to Leah. "As I mentioned before, my friend decided to get out of farming after her pet chicken died. I promised her these last two were going to a good home."

Laverne inched closer.

One of the chickens scrambled toward her. *BOK...BOK.*

She stumbled back, clutching her chest.

"This one is a little twitchy," Carrie said. "I don't think she liked riding in the car."

"She looks evil. Do you see how she's staring at me?"

It did look as if the bird was eyeing Laverne.

"Maybe you scared her," Jo said.

"You might want to let them out of the cage. Wendy said they like to explore new surroundings. It helps them become more comfortable."

Leah turned to Jo, seeking her approval.

"They're your hens."

Leah lifted the latch and opened the door. "You can come out," she coaxed in a soft voice.

One of them strutted forward. The hen lingered in the doorway for a fraction of a second before lightly stepping onto the gravel driveway.

The second one followed behind and then hovered near the entrance, their heads bobbing up and down as they eyed their new surroundings.

"I think they like it here," Leah said excitedly.

Gary grinned. "Leah finally got those chickens. I can't wait to see how they like their new home."

Leah let them explore the grassy area before scooping one up and placing it back inside the cage. She reached for the second one, who skittered just out of reach. "Come here, chicky-chicky," she sing-songed.

She lunged forward, but the bird was too fast. She let out a loud *BOK*.

The hen on the lam made a beeline for Laverne.

Laverne darted left.

The hen mirrored her move.

Laverne bolted to the right. The hen rushed forward, loudly squawking as it closed in on her.

"That demon bird is after me!" she screeched.

"I don't..."

The bird squawked again, furiously flapping its wings as it bore down on the woman.

Laverne pivoted, taking off at a dead run.

The chase was on as the hen ran after her.

Laverne wrapped both arms around her head as the hen flew forward with surprising speed. Seconds later, the bird dive-bombed Laverne, knocking her to the ground.

Chapter 7

Jo dashed across the yard to where Laverne lay sprawled out on the ground. Her egg-laying attacker was mere feet away, calmly clucking and strutting.

Leah snatched the bird up and whisked it back to the cage while Jo dropped to her knees. "Are you all right?"

Laverne let out a low groan as she rolled onto her back. "The crazed animal attacked me."

"It does appear that one of Leah's hens doesn't like you."

Carrie tottered over. "I had no idea the chicken would react like that."

"Someone needs to chop that thing's head off, pluck out her feathers, and fry her up for dinner." Laverne grimaced as she lightly touched the back of her head. When she pulled her hand away, there was blood on the tips of her fingers. "The bugger drew blood."

"I'm...I'm sorry you were injured, but you can't be serious about killing the chicken. I promised Wendy no harm would come to either of them."

"We're not going to kill the chickens." Jo extended a hand and helped Laverne to her feet. "Has your friend ever mentioned the chicken attacking anyone before?"

"Once. It was a door-to-door salesperson. He never came back."

"I need to put something on this. Who knows what kinds of diseases it could be carrying." Laverne limped around to the back of the building.

"I'll grab some peroxide and run it over to her," Delta said.

"Thanks, Delta. I'll swing by to check on her after Carrie leaves."

"I feel so bad about the hen attacking Laverne." Carrie pressed a finger to her lips as Delta hurried off. "You don't think she'll follow through on the threat and harm the hen, do you?"

"She won't. You have my word."

Leah rounded the side of the barn, carrying the empty carrier, and handed it to Carrie. "The hens like their new home."

"I'm sure they do." Carrie placed the metal cage in the back of her minivan and dusted her hands as she turned to Jo. "I heard about Barnaby Iteen's body being found out behind Gary's barn."

"Actually, Duke found him." Jo briefly told her the story, how the hound had been chasing the neighbor's chickens. When she and Delta caught up with him, he was standing next to the well.

"He wasn't a very nice man." Carrie made a cross sign. "God rest his soul."

"You knew him?"

"My Abner used to hang out with Barnaby over at the Half Wall Bar. Him and Sonny Pabst, another local." Carrie glanced around and lowered her voice. "Barnaby couldn't stand Gary after Gary turned him in to the authorities."

"For theft," Jo said. "From what I've been told, Gary wasn't the only one."

"Oh no." Carrie's eyes grew wide. "Barnaby made his rounds, working here and there, but he always managed to get into some sort of trouble. I figured he finally left town after cheating one too many people. He also liked to drink a lot and shoot off his mouth."

"Do you mean that he picked fights?"

"No, with Barnaby, it was more like a 'loose lips sink ships' type of thing."

"Can you think of anyone who may have disliked him enough to kill him?" Jo asked.

"Not off the top of my head. I do know someone who might...Florence Parlow, the owner of Half Wall Bar."

"Marlee mentioned the same thing, how he hung out there and picked up some of his odd jobs from people he met at the bar."

"Flo knows a lot. Like I said, Barnaby was a regular. He was also friends with Rick something, another regular, and Charlie Golden."

"Who is Charlie Golden?" Jo had yet to hear that name.

"He's the caretaker over at Centerpoint's landmark."

Jo thanked Carrie for the information as she followed the woman to the driver's side.

"You don't think Delta is going to call off the wedding now that people suspect Gary might be a killer, do you?"

"Gary didn't kill Barnaby."

"That's not what I'm hearing around town. I mean, not that I believe it." Carrie slid behind the wheel. She pulled the door shut and rolled the window down. "I try not to pay too much attention to the gossip. I know most of it's made up. Look at the false information circulating out there about me."

Carrie had a point. She also had a reputation around the small town of Divine. The most persistent was she was a little kooky. Jo thought a more appropriate description was "unique." Regardless of Carrie's history and some eccentric tendencies, she had been a loyal friend to Jo and the residents, which was all that mattered.

After she was gone, Jo headed into the house. Delta was in the kitchen. She cast a glance over her shoulder but didn't pause as she continued pounding the cutting board.

"What are you making?"

"Italian chicken rollups."

Intrigued, Jo made her way over, watching as Delta hammered away at a chicken breast. "Can I help?"

"Sure. I need thinly sliced red onion and some chopped green olives."

After gathering the ingredients, Jo set them on the counter and began working on slicing the onion first.

"Did Leah finally manage to corral those crazy chickens?"

"Yeah. I don't think we'll be putting Laverne in charge of chicken coop duty anytime soon."

"Those chickens are smart," Delta said. "They know a rotten egg when they see it."

"C'mon, Delta." Jo chuckled. "Laverne isn't all that bad."

"I was joking. The hen managed to get Laverne pretty good." Delta was silent for a moment. "I'm sure Carrie had plenty to say about Barnaby Iteen's death."

"She did. She claims Barnaby used to hang out with her husband at Half Wall Bar."

"Florence's bar is almost as popular as Marlee's deli." Delta grabbed two large glass baking dishes and placed them on the counter. "I haven't stepped foot inside that place in decades. In fact, I can't even recall who owned it back in the day. It wasn't Florence Parlow, I do know that."

Jo finished chopping the onions and olives. "What's next?"

"Pepperoni, Italian cheese and pizza sauce from the fridge."

The women began assembling the Italian rollups. The first layer was pepperoni, followed by a generous layer of cheese. Jo sprinkled the chopped olives and sliced onions on top before rolling the chicken up.

Her first attempt was lopsided, but by the second one, she'd gotten the hang of it. The women made quick work of assembling them. After finishing, Delta spread sauce across the top, followed by more cheese, before sliding the dishes into the preheated oven. "Easy peasy dinner for a crowd."

"I can't wait to try them." While Jo cleaned the kitchen, Delta whipped up a tossed salad and then began loading frozen breadsticks onto empty cookie sheets. "I know you've been itching to ask me what I think about Barnaby's death and the fact Gary had hired him at one time."

"I'll confess, I'm a little curious to hear your thoughts."

Delta set the salad in the fridge and turned her attention to her friend. "I'm as loyal a person as they come."

"You are," Jo agreed. "You're the best. I couldn't even imagine running this place without you."

"I wouldn't be true to myself if I bailed on Gary now. I love him. He loves me. I'm gonna stick by my man."

"And he would do the same."

"Yes, he would."

Jo gave her a thumbs up. "I want to check on Laverne. While we're at it, we can talk to her about your wedding cake."

With plenty of time before the rollups finished baking, they walked next door to the women's common area. They found Laverne curled up on the couch, holding an ice pack to the back of her head.

"How are you feeling?" Jo made her way around the side.

"Like I've been attacked by Alfred Hitchcock's, *The Birds*." Laverne winced as she removed the bag of ice. "I think that crazy bird almost pecked through my skull."

"Let me have a look." Jo gently parted Laverne's hair and inspected the now dried blood.

Delta joined her, and they both peered at Laverne's injury. "It's a little worse than I originally thought. I have some ointment at the house we can put on it to make sure the wound doesn't get infected."

"Thanks." Laverne waited for Delta to depart. "I heard Gary knew the guy whose body was found on his property. Is she gonna dump him now that he's a suspect?"

"No. Delta is not going to dump him. The deceased wasn't an upstanding citizen. Besides, we don't know how he died. He could very well have died of natural causes."

"Right." Laverne looked skeptical. "And he just happened to have died right there behind Gary's barn, not to mention figured out a way to bury himself before doing so."

Jo started to reply, but Delta returned, effectively ending their conversation.

"I'll put a little dab of this on the wound." Delta opened the tube and dabbed a generous amount on the back of Laverne's head. "What did you do to get that hen all riled up in the first place?"

"I don't know. Maybe I looked at it the wrong way. Farm critters don't like me. Never have. Probably never will."

"We'll be sure to keep coop cleaning or egg gathering off your list of jobs," Jo promised. "The other reason we're here is to discuss the wedding cake."

"Finally," Laverne said. "Since you were non-committal, Gary decided on a traditional cake. Based on the color of your dress, I say we go with silver and white."

"But no woman dragging her man off the top," Delta said.

"No fun cake topping." Laverne pursed her lips. "It will be your boring, run-of-the-mill cake."

The trio gathered at the table to go over the details. Jo was secretly pleased to see the two, who had butted heads from day one, working together.

They wrapped up the details, and then Delta and Jo returned to the house to begin the final meal preparations. The Italian rollups finished last, and Jo helped by carrying platters of food to the dining room, greeting the residents as they each took their spot at the table.

When everyone, minus Gary, had assembled, they bowed their heads, and Jo began to pray. "Dear Heavenly Father. Thank you for the bountiful food on our table. We thank you for all of our blessings, for our health. Lord, we pray for peace not only for our household but for Delta and Gary as their wedding day grows closer." She ended it, thanking God for his Son, their Savior. "Amen."

"Amen," the table's occupants echoed.

"This looks delicious." Jo, who hadn't had a chance to sample the dish, eagerly placed one of the rollups on her plate. She spread a generous spoonful of sauce along the top before passing the serving dish to Nash.

She added a breadstick before slicing off a small piece of the rollup. Her mouth watered as she scraped up a chunk of melted cheese before taking her first bite. The cheese was gooey, and the onion, mixed with the olive and pepperoni, tickled her tastebuds. "It tastes every bit as good as I thought it would."

"Delta, you've outdone yourself," Raylene murmured. "What is this?"

"Thanks." Delta beamed. "They're baked Italian chicken rollups." She rattled off the ingredients.

"Sorry that I'm late." Gary stepped into the dining room and took his seat next to Delta. "I was checking on the hens."

"No need to apologize."

Gary set his napkin in his lap and added two rollups to his plate before passing the platter to Leah, who was sitting on his left. "Is this the rollup recipe you've been talking about trying?"

"It is." Delta's soon-to-be husband wasted no time polishing off the first rollup. "This is darned near as good as your hot Italian pesto pasta dish," he complimented.

"And fairly easy to make," Jo chimed in. "Thanks to Laverne, Delta has finalized the plans for the wedding cake.

"I have the artificial flowers in the works," Kelli chimed in.

While they ate, they discussed the details of the much-anticipated celebration. Meanwhile, Gary spent most of the time quietly eating his food.

During dessert, Jo brought up the subject of the hens, directing her question to Leah. "How are the hens settling in?"

"Great. They love Gary's chicken coop."

"I'll have to check it out later."

"I've been trying to think of names for them."

"How about dead?" Laverne joked.

"I'm not naming either of my chickens dead."

"How about naming one of them Barbecue?"

"My hens are for eggs, not to eat." Leah's face turned red. "I'm sorry you were attacked, but it wasn't the hen's fault."

"Then whose fault was it?"

"She was scared. It was a defense mechanism."

"By chasing me down and pecking my skull?"

Jo held up a hand. "Caring for the hens will not be one of Laverne's duties. I think Henrietta is a cute name."

The women all threw out different ideas. Leah picked Jo's suggestion along with Kelli's name, Egglina.

Gary abruptly shoved his chair back and stood. "I think I'm gonna head home. It's been a long day."

Delta followed suit. "I'll walk you out."

"We'll clean up." Jo shooed them out of the dining room and waited until she heard the front porch door slam shut. "Let's give them some privacy."

While the women began clearing the dishes, Nash pulled Jo aside. "Something's up."

"Gary was very quiet during dinner," Jo said in a low voice.

"I tried talking to him before we came over for dinner. He barely spoke five words to me."

"I'm sure he's stressed out. The wedding. The body."

The conversation ended when Leah returned to wipe the table.

After finishing the cleanup, the women exited through the back porch door, leaving Nash and Jo alone in the kitchen.

"Dinner was delicious."

"It was. Delta comes up with some of the most amazing recipes." Jo folded her arms and leaned her hip against the counter. "I don't know how we'll survive while she and Gary are on their honeymoon."

"You could let Laverne have a crack at cooking for us," Nash joked.

"Don't think I haven't considered it. The only problem is the attempted kitchen takeover I'm envisioning. Delta won't have it."

"True. Maybe it's best to keep Laverne away." Nash slipped his arm around Jo's waist and pulled her close. "I'll be sure to come over here and spend my evenings with you while you're home alone."

"I'll be home alone from their wedding day forward."

"I like the sound of that." Nash lowered his head, his lips gently touching Jo's. She wrapped her arms around his neck, her heart pitter-pattering as he pulled her even closer.

Finally, Nash lifted his head, his eyes smoldering. "I would apologize, but I'm not sorry."

"I'm not sorry, either." Jo pressed a hand to her flushed cheeks.

There was a muffled sound coming from the doorway, and they quickly stepped apart, catching a glimpse of Delta, who was standing in the doorway.

"I'm sorry. I didn't mean to interrupt."

A slow smile spread across Nash's face. "It's probably best that you did."

Jo playfully punched him in the arm. "Very funny." She turned her attention to Delta. "Did Gary leave?"

"Yeah. Gary's gone." Delta trudged across the kitchen in the direction of her bedroom.

Jo, sensing something was wrong, hurried after her. "Is everything all right?"

Delta stopped in the hallway, her back stiffening as she stared straight ahead. "No. Not really."

Chapter 8

"Gary called off the wedding."

Jo's jaw dropped. "He *what*?"

"He called off the wedding. I'm going to bed." Delta stepped inside her bedroom, closing the door behind her. Jo started to follow, but Nash stopped her. "It's probably best if we give her a little space."

"This is awful."

Nash consulted his watch. "Maybe they had some sort of misunderstanding. I'm going to head over to Gary's house."

Jo walked him to the front door and stood on the porch, watching as he ran up to his apartment. He returned moments later and climbed into his pickup. She said a silent prayer, watching as his taillights faded in the distance.

Back inside, she made her way into the kitchen and hall where Delta's bedroom was located. Her door was still closed, and Jo could tell the lights were off.

A feeling of helplessness filled her. She paced the floor before finally grabbing her cell phone and heading back out to the porch. She caught a glimpse of light flash from the vicinity of the garden shed. Duke, who had joined Jo, let out a warning growl.

Casting a furtive glance around, she cautiously followed Duke across the driveway. She caught up with him near the shed. Leah was inside, her back to them as she filled a watering can.

Jo gave the door a light rap, and Leah spun around. "Oh. Hi, Jo."

"Duke and I saw your light and decided to investigate. What're you doing?"

"Checking on the hens. I want to make sure they've settled in for the night."

"Maybe you should've asked Gary to build their coop closer to your apartment," Jo teased.

Leah grinned. "Are you kidding? Laverne would freak out."

"True."

The women fell into step as they made their way around back. "Thanks again for letting me get hens."

"You're welcome. If things go well, perhaps we'll add more."

The hens began clucking loudly as the women drew near but quickly quieted when Leah began talking to them, making cooing sounds. She refilled the watering station and tiptoed out, closing the door behind her.

"I do believe you're the chicken whisperer."

"I can't wait to start collecting eggs. It's probably best if Laverne doesn't care for the hens. They don't seem to like her." Leah shifted the watering can to her other hand. "I'm a little worried about Gary." She confided in Jo that he had seemed distracted and barely talked all afternoon.

"He has a lot on his mind."

"About the man's body that they found at his place," Leah guessed.

"Yes."

"Gary didn't do anything to him."

"No, he didn't." Jo sighed heavily. "I'm sure the authorities will sort it out soon." At least she hoped they would. "You mentioned Laverne. How's it going with our newest resident?"

"She's okay. She can be a little bossy, but she tries to be helpful too."

"I get the same impression. How do you think the others feel about her?"

"Ditto. We've actually talked about it. We miss Sherry. It's different now that she's moved out."

"I miss Sherry too."

"I know she's busy, but it would be nice if she stopped by more often."

"I'll give her a call and invite her to dinner," Jo promised.

Back inside the shed, she waited for Leah to take care of the watering supplies and parted ways with her in the driveway as she and Duke returned to the porch. She dialed Sherry's cell phone, expecting the call to go to voice mail. Instead, her former resident answered. "Hi, Jo."

"Hey, Sherry. Leah and I were just talking about you, so I thought I would give you a call. How is everything?"

"Great." There was a clattering sound on the other end of the line.

"What are you doing?" Jo asked.

"Fixing dinner for Todd and me."

"Todd, as in your neighbor, Todd?"

"Yep. He stopped by my apartment the other day to check on me. We got to talking, and I offered to make him dinner."

"Now that you mention dinner, I called to invite you to join us perhaps one day next week."

"Let me take a look at my work schedule, and I'll get back to you."

"Sounds good. I won't keep you." Jo started to say good-bye, and Sherry stopped her. "I'm off tomorrow morning if you would like to stop by."

"I'll do that." Jo promised to give her a call in the morning before hanging up. She hung out on the porch, waiting for Nash to return from Gary's place before finally giving up and turning in.

It was a restless night as Jo tossed and turned, worrying about Delta and Gary. She thought about Raylene's upcoming visit from Aaron Beck and wondered why he had contacted her out of the blue after all of these years.

She woke early the next morning, still groggy but unable to go back to sleep. She finally crawled out of bed and headed downstairs.

Delta was seated at the kitchen table, a cup of coffee and plate of donuts in front of her. She gave Jo a passing glance as she took a big bite of an éclair.

"Your donut looks good."

"There's plenty to go around."

Jo grabbed a coffee cup from the counter, noticing the pot was already half empty. "You've been up for a while."

"You could say that. I've been here long enough to eat my daily calories in one sitting. This is my fourth donut."

Jo refilled her friend's cup. On her way back to the table, she grabbed a knife. She sliced a cinnamon donut in half and took a big bite. "Have you heard from Gary since last night?"

"Nope. I've been thinking, maybe this whole Barnaby Iteen thing is for the best. I mean, not that he died, certainly, but maybe this is God's way of preventing Gary and me from making a big mistake."

Jo wrinkled her nose as she took another bite.

"I'm serious. This could be a blessing in disguise. Besides, Gary has every right to get cold feet. I did."

"True." Jo thought about Delta's list of reasons about why she should or shouldn't marry Gary. Maybe she was right. Perhaps neither of them was ready, both being older and set in their ways. Perhaps there had been warning signs Jo hadn't noticed.

There was a light knock on the back porch door. "I'll get it." Jo shoved the rest of the donut in her mouth and scrambled down the steps. She peeked out the window and found Nash standing on the other side.

"Hey, Jo. I'm sorry to bother you so early," he said sheepishly.

"It's no bother. Delta and I were chatting and chowing down on donuts. Come join us."

Nash followed Jo into the kitchen and greeted Delta. "Morning, Delta."

"Coffee?" Jo poured a cup and handed it to him.

"Thanks. I came by to tell you Gary won't be coming into work today."

Delta swung around. "So, he's quitting his job and dumping his bride-to-be at the same time?"

Nash shifted uncomfortably. "He blames himself for Iteen's death. He broke off the engagement so you wouldn't be stuck with a man who'll always be suspected of murdering someone. Same for the job. Gary is insisting Jo has to deal with enough flak from the locals and doesn't want to pile on his problems."

"You mean he wasn't trying to back out of our marriage? He thinks he's protecting me?"

"He's trying to shield you from suspicion and speculation. He doesn't want you to be saddled with him and his problems."

Delta's eyes sparked as she slammed her hand on the table. "That's foolish. Why I'm a grown woman. Nobody's gonna accuse me of turning into a namby-pamby."

"Gary is worth fighting for. Your marriage is worth fighting for. Maybe you should go talk to him, try to clear the air," Jo said.

"Darn tootin'." Delta shoved her chair back and marched out of the room.

Nash arched a brow. "That lit her up."

Delta returned a short time later. "It's settled. The wedding is back on. Gary will be here within the hour. I told him I wasn't giving up on him and that we are going to get to the bottom of what happened to Barnaby Iteen."

"Good for you." Jo shook her fist. "That's the spirit. That's the Delta I know and love."

Delta's resolve quickly faded. "I can talk a big talk, but now what?"

"It's time to crack a cold case. Our first step is to start doing some digging around. From what Carrie told me, Barnaby wasn't exactly an upstanding citizen. He made his share of enemies, committed enough crimes to possibly make someone mad — maybe even mad enough to take him out."

"And dump his body on Gary's property," Nash added.

"We need to prove Gary wasn't involved even though he had both motive and opportunity." Jo tapped her chin thoughtfully. "It would be easy enough for him to be set up. But by who?"

Delta rubbed a weary hand over her brow. "I don't even know where to begin."

"Don't get discouraged. Based on what Carrie told me yesterday, I know exactly where we need to start."

Chapter 9

It didn't take long for Jo to convince Delta that if they wanted to get to the bottom of what exactly had happened to Barnaby Iteen, they needed to start at the place where he hung out.

But first, she'd promised Sherry she would stop by after breakfast. When Delta found out, she flew into action, whipping up a breakfast bake for the residents and a second, smaller one for Sherry.

She threw together a pasta dish, adding a brief instruction sheet. For good measure, she made a batch of morning glory muffins, one of Sherry's favorites.

Gary arrived for breakfast a few minutes early, looking embarrassed. Thankfully, the residents didn't seem to notice. Even Delta acted as if the previous night had never happened.

As soon as the meal ended, Jo and Delta packed up the food and made the short drive into town.

Jo had given Sherry a heads up they were on their way, and she was waiting for them in the parking lot. "That was fast."

Delta hugged Sherry tightly before reaching back inside the SUV for the bags of food.

"What's this?"

"Enough food to last a week," Jo joked.

"Delta." Sherry wagged her finger. "You didn't have to bring me food."

"No food?" Delta feigned a look of horror. "I can't arrive at my favorite gal's home empty-handed."

"This is a real treat. Thank you." Sherry led them to her upstairs apartment. "Can I make you a cup of coffee or tea?"

"No, thanks. Jo and I have been up for hours. We're all coffee-d out."

Jo watched as Sherry put the goodies away. "So, how did dinner with Todd go?"

"Let's just say that my meatloaf and mashed potatoes were edible. I need to work on my cooking skills. I think Todd's lonely. He hasn't met anyone in town."

"Mmm. Hmm." Delta shot her a sly grin. "Do I detect a possible romance brewing?"

"Not even. Todd has a girlfriend. She lives in California and will be coming to Divine for a visit soon."

"Long-distance romances don't last."

"I don't know the status of their relationship, whether it's serious or not. All I know is that he has a girlfriend." Sherry changed the subject. "Miles stopped by the deli yesterday to drop off a ticket for his theater's grand opening."

"Oh?" Jo lifted a brow.

"I run into him almost every day when I'm on my way to the bank to deposit my tip money. He's a nice guy."

"And single, as well."

Sherry's cheeks turned a tinge of pink, and Jo sensed she was making the woman uncomfortable. "He gave me tickets for everyone at the farm too. You're welcome to sit with us."

"He, uh. He also gave me a VIP pass to join him in the owner's booth." Sherry hurried on. "I won't be the only one. He's invited some others as well."

"I see." Jo let it drop, uncertain how she felt about Miles, her half-brother, and her former resident showing an interest in each other. Although, technically, it wasn't any of her business. Sherry was a free agent and no longer under Jo's watchful eye.

The trio discussed the wedding and Sherry's job. Finally, Jo reluctantly stood. "We need to get going."

"Thank you for coming over." Sherry followed them back downstairs. "Since I'm not scheduled to work until this afternoon, I was thinking about maybe stopping by the farm to see everyone."

Jo jingled her keys. "We'll be going back that way – sort of. Would you like us to drop you off? Nash or Gary can run you home later."

Sherry brightened. "Could you?"

"Absolutely. Go grab your things and lock up."

Delta and Jo waited in the vehicle while Sherry dashed upstairs to grab her purse.

During the ride to the farm, she chattered about how much she loved her apartment, how she'd met some locals who were opening a coffee bar in one of the empty buildings on Main Street, among other things.

Back home, Jo circled around and stopped near the entrance to the bakeshop. Sherry sprang from the vehicle. With a hasty good-bye, she hurried into the building.

Delta tugged on her seatbelt. "The others are gonna be so excited to see Sherry."

"It's good for the residents to see firsthand how well she's doing. She's a great role model." Since Jo had no idea how to get to Half Wall Bar, she relied on Delta for directions. It was farther out than she'd realized.

Finally, they reached their destination. The gravel parking lot was empty except for a conversion van parked off to the side.

"This place looks abandoned." Delta exited the SUV and waited for Jo on the sidewalk. According to the sign on the door, the bar had just opened.

They stepped inside where the pungent aroma of stale cigarette smoke lingered in the air. Jo shifted her gaze, taking in the dark paneling and stained yellow curtains hanging on the small windows.

A long bar with a woman standing behind it was on the left-hand side. Her cropped locks spiked up in the back. A row of bangs covered her forehead.

"Morning, ladies." She leaned an elbow on the counter, eyeing them with interest as they approached the bar.

"Good morning." Jo extended her hand. "I'm Joanna Pepperdine, owner of Second Chance Mercantile and Divine Bake Shop."

"Joanna Pepperdine," the woman repeated. "I know who you are. You run that halfway house for female convicts."

"Former female convicts," Jo corrected.

"Right. You sure did ruffle a few feathers in the area when you moved here." The woman chuckled as she shook Jo's hand. "Florence Parlow, owner of this fine establishment. Most people 'round here call me Flo."

"Flo. My pleasure." Jo climbed onto a nearby barstool. "Since we're patronizing your business, I'll take a Sprite, light on the ice."

"Ditto." Delta joined her. "Except I like a lot of ice."

"Two Sprites, coming right up." Florence reached for the glasses. "I'm gonna take a wild guess and say you're not really here for a Sprite."

"We're here to ask you about Barnaby Iteen," Jo said.

Flo abruptly stopped with the ice scooper mid-air. "I heard they found Barnaby, or what was left of him, over at Gary Stein's place."

"Gary works for me, and he's a friend of mine. I'm trying to figure out what happened to Mr. Iteen."

"Now, that might be tricky." The woman placed two napkins on the bar and set the drinks on top. "Barnaby had his share of troubles."

The door's bell tinkled, and a man, heavyset and in his sixties, if Jo had to guess, wearing a three-piece suit strolled in.

Florence acknowledged his arrival with a nod of her head. "Pabst."

"Am I too late for happy hour?" the man joked.

"Never too late for you. I'll be right over."
Florence dusted her hands. "Where were we? Yeah,
Barnaby. He was well-acquainted with the county
sheriff. Trouble seemed to follow him wherever he
went."

"So, he made some enemies," Delta said.

"Most certainly. I don't know Stein, but I know
that he hired Barnaby to do some work for him, and
then he caught him stealing stuff. Stein fired him
and filed a police report."

"We've heard the same." Jo sipped her Sprite.
"We also heard this was his hangout and wondered
if you knew of anyone who might have had it in for
him."

Florence rattled off a list of first names. "Those
are only a few off the top of my head. Let's just say
whoever Barnaby worked for ended up having some
sort of issue."

The man at the other end of the bar hollered down. "You talking about Barnaby?"

"It's nothing, Sonny. I'll be right there." Flo lowered her voice. "One day, he up and disappeared." The bar's phone rang, and she hurried off to answer it.

The man in the suit joined them. "I knew Barnaby."

"Mr. Iteen was found on a friend's property. We're trying to figure out what exactly happened to him."

"And you are..."

"Joanna Pepperdine."

"No kidding." The man shoved his hands in his pockets, giving Jo his full attention. "I've heard your name before. You bought the old McDougall place and filled it with former convicts."

"I wouldn't say five women is a farm full, but yes, they do reside on my property." She waited for what she suspected was coming next and was pleasantly surprised when the man thanked her for helping those who needed a hand up. "I gotta say, you have more guts than I do."

"Perhaps not guts but compassion." Jo changed the subject. "So, you knew Mr. Iteen, Mr...."

"Pabst. Sonny Pabst. We used to meet up here at the bar a coupla times a week." Sonny Pabst told Jo when Barnaby first blew into town, he started hearing the rumors that Iteen was trouble. "I like to judge a man on his merits and by my own personal dealings, not to mention there are some people around here who don't like outsiders. Iteen was an outsider."

"I can't disagree with you there."

Sonny rubbed the stubble on his chin. "My buddy, Rick, had a run-in with him."

"Rick?"

"Rick Pringle, the owner of Pringle Construction."

Flo finished her call and returned to the bar. "Are you here to have a beer or socialize?"

Pabst rapped his knuckles on the counter. "You know me, Flo. I'll take the usual." He turned to go. "Even Florence, here, had a run-in with old Iteen."

She reached into the cooler and grabbed a mug. "Along with everyone else."

Jo's scalp tingled. Florence had mentioned others who had run-ins with Barnaby but so far hadn't mentioned her own.

"Besides, I've tossed more than Barnaby out of my bar for causing trouble."

"That's true." Pabst loosened his necktie. "If you're looking for information on Barnaby, I suggest you pay a visit to Charlie Golden over at Centerpoint's chapel."

"Charlie Golden." Jo remembered hearing Carrie mention his name.

"He's the caretaker. He and Barnaby were poker buddies, at least that's what Barnaby claimed. Charlie might have some thoughts on what happened to him."

"Sonny." Florence handed him the frosted mug. "You know how I feel about spreading rumors."

"And anything about Dex."

"Leave Dexter out of this. He didn't have a beef with Barnaby." Flo gave him a warning look before heading to the trio of men who had just arrived.

Sonny started to say something but abruptly stopped. "Florence is right. I shouldn't have said anything." He mumbled something under his breath and excused himself before resuming his spot at the other end of the bar.

Flo returned. "I make a mean burger if you're ever in the mood to stop by for lunch."

"Yes, we'll have to do that," Jo politely replied. She and Delta hurriedly finished their sodas and exited the bar. "Well? What do you think?"

"I think Sonny was going to say something, and Florence stopped him," Delta said. "Did you see the look she gave him?"

"She got upset when he mentioned the name Dex." Jo checked the rearview mirror before backing up. "It looks like we're heading to our next stop, Divine's claim to fame."

Once again, Delta played navigator, giving Jo road-by-road directions past miles of rolling farm fields for as far as the eye could see.

They turned onto a narrow two-lane road that branched off and narrowed even more. Off in the distance, Jo spotted a chapel steeple.

She turned into the parking area and peered through the windshield. "I visited this place once, but I don't remember it being this far out."

Delta reached for the door handle. "Just between you and me, I never could figure out what all the fuss was about and why this place attracts so many visitors."

"I, for one, am thrilled that it does." On closer inspection, Jo discovered there wasn't much to the spot, except for the small chapel, some picnic tables, and a stone monument.

The chapel was tiny – not much bigger than an oversized storage shed. The exterior consisted of white siding, and the trim was a light gray. A white steeple with a cross on top was above the door, and bright blue flowered curtains hung from the windows.

They approached the front entrance, and Jo could see the door was ajar. She pressed lightly on the frame, easing it open.

The chapel was empty. Wooden pews lined both sides of the narrow aisle, an oak lectern was front and center. The floor creaked as the women followed an earthy aroma to the front of the room.

Jo wandered over to inspect the contents of a small corner shelf. A black box, a guest registry and a pen were on top. She jotted her name down and handed the pen to Delta.

"What's this?" She reached for the box, not realizing it was bolted to the shelf.

"I dunno." Delta carefully printed her name and set the pen on top before tapping the side of the box.

"Hey," a male voice echoed from the door.

Jo clutched her chest and spun around. A man with his hulking frame blocking their only way out filled the doorway.

Chapter 10

"What are you doing with the donation box?" The man took a menacing step toward them.

"Donation box?" Delta snatched her hand back. "We were trying to figure out what it was."

"How did you get in here?"

"The door was unlocked," Jo said.

"Unlocked and ajar," Delta added. "I thought this place was open to the public."

"It was until a bunch of riffraff recently started targeting the chapel."

"I can assure you it wasn't us." Jo straightened her back. "If we were messing around, we certainly wouldn't park our vehicle out front."

The man apologized and introduced himself. "I'm Charlie Golden, the caretaker."

"Ah." Jo let out a sigh of relief. "That makes sense."

"Not only am I the caretaker of this fine establishment, but I'm also a member of the preservation society." While Charlie talked, he began lightly tapping the walls.

Curiosity got the better of Jo. "What are you doing?"

"It's part of my daily routine. I once read that if you tap on walls, it wards off evil spirits." He rapped all four walls before returning to the exit.

Jo removed a ten-dollar bill from her wallet and placed it in the donation box. "Actually, you're the reason why we're here."

"Me?"

"We just left the Half Wall Bar and were told you might be able to help us."

"So, you're not here to visit the chapel?"

"No," Jo admitted. "But it is a lovely place. I don't know anything about its history."

Charlie's face lit up. "You live in the area and don't know anything about our famous landmark? If you have a minute, I'll show you around."

"That would be wonderful," Jo said.

"We'll start our tour down yonder." Charlie led them past the pavilion and up a small hill. When they reached the top, he abruptly stopped. "Check out those clouds."

Jo followed his gaze. "It's a beautiful day."

Golden dropped to his knees and gave the ground a tentative sniff.

Delta and Jo exchanged a quick glance.

"Is there something wrong?" Delta asked.

"I need to mow, but first, I want to make sure it's not going to rain." Charlie plucked a blade of grass and rolled it between his fingers. "There won't be any rain today, but a storm's brewing."

"You can tell that a storm's brewing just by sniffing the ground and rolling grass between your fingers?" Jo asked.

"Yes, ma'am. I'm a self-taught naturalist." He sprang to his feet and began walking again, with Delta and Jo hustling to keep up with his pace. "Nature speaks. I listen."

"You said a storm is brewing," Delta prompted.

"A bad one. I've been checking the wind direction all morning." Charlie licked the tip of his finger and held it up. "Hasn't changed. I'll bet money a supercell or even supercells are on the way."

Jo contemplated his ominous prediction. Their spring and early summer season had spawned several tornadoes in recent weeks. The weather forecasters were predicting an active and deadly season. "I hope you're wrong."

"Could be, but probably not," Charlie said. "We'll find out soon enough."

Headstones dotted the landscape at the bottom of the incline, and towering oak trees surrounded the cemetery. A rutted track meandered around the perimeter.

A gentle breeze rolled across the valley, blowing Jo's hair into her eyes. She smoothed it back as she surveyed the peaceful surroundings. "This is a lovely spot for a cemetery."

"It is. In fact, I have my own plot down yonder." They descended the small hill as Charlie continued talking. "The cemetery is at capacity, and the county officials voted down any expansion."

The trio stepped onto the dirt path and circled around the side until they reached the back corner.

It had been years since Jo's last visit to a cemetery – not since her mother's death. She'd thought about visiting her parents' gravesites a number of times but couldn't bring herself to actually follow through.

Even now, gazing at the tombstones filled her with an overwhelming sense of loss. Without warning, she had a momentary flashback of her mother's graveside service. Jo gave herself a mental shake. She needed to stay focused.

They finished the tour where they began, in the parking lot not far from Jo's SUV. "Thank you for the tour."

"You're welcome. You mentioned needing my help."

"Skeletal remains were found on Gary Stein's property a couple days ago."

"No kidding." The look of surprise on Charlie's face was genuine. "Human remains?"

"Yes. Does the name Barnaby Iteen ring a bell?" Jo asked.

Golden's jaw dropped. "Barnaby's dead?"

"For some time now. We were told you and Barnaby were friends."

"We were. To put it mildly, Barnaby wasn't real popular 'round these parts. People spread stories about him. Some were true. Some weren't."

"Did he ever mention fearing for his life?"

"Nope, but then Barnaby ran with a rough crowd." Charlie scratched his forehead. "Now that I think about it, the last time I saw him, he said he was working on a big deal, something that was going to bring him some cash."

"Did he mention who he was working with?" Delta asked.

"Not that I can recall. He did say he was keeping his information in a safe place."

When pressed, Charlie couldn't remember much else about Barnaby's "big deal." "Could've been just about anything. He worked a few jobs around the area but never anything permanent. He was always getting into hot water for one reason or another. I felt sorry for him and hired him to mow the grass a few times. He wasn't particularly reliable. He liked

147

to spend more time hanging out over at Half Wall Bar than making an honest day's living. Maybe you should talk to Rick Pringle."

Jo remembered hearing someone at the bar mention the name. "Rick Pringle," she repeated.

"He owns Pringle Construction. At one time, Rick and Sonny Pabst were buddies with Barnaby." Golden kicked at a rock with the tip of his work boot. "I still can't believe Barnaby's gone. I figured he'd high-tailed it out of town."

"Sonny said you and Barnaby liked to play poker."

Charlie spewed a string of swear words and then spat on the ground. "Sonny's a liar."

A wave of fear washed over Jo at the sudden change in the caretaker's demeanor. Her eyes darted around. Two women all alone in the middle of nowhere. "I...we should get going."

"I didn't mean to go off on you," Charlie apologized. "I'm not a huge fan of Pabst. Rick's either. I'm sure Pabst was probably deep in his drink when he was shooting off his mouth."

"It could be," Jo agreed.

Charlie glanced at his watch. "If you'll excuse me, daylight is burning, and I have a lot of lawn to mow." He turned on his heel and stalked off across the parking lot.

"Let's go," Jo muttered under her breath.

"While the getting is good."

They climbed into the SUV, and Jo locked the doors before starting the vehicle. "First impressions?"

Delta twirled her finger next to her forehead. "He's an odd man – tapping walls and sniffing dirt. Did you see how angry he got when we mentioned Pabst and playing poker?"

"I caught that too," Jo said. "I'm on the fence about the guy. He seems a bit eccentric, but perhaps he's harmless."

Delta shrugged. "Or maybe it's an act."

Jo slid her purse between the door and her seat. It tipped over, and her cell phone fell out. "Crud." She snatched it off the floor and started to place it back inside when she noticed she'd missed a call. "Nash called. He left a message."

She drove out of the chapel's parking lot and waited until they were a safe distance away before pulling off the road. She entered her six-digit access code before listening to the message. "Uh-oh."

"Uh-oh, what?"

"Listen to this." Jo hit the speaker button and then played the message a second time.

"Hey, Jo. Nash here. You and Delta might want to head home. I take that back. You might want to head over to Gary's place." Nash rattled off the time before ending the call.

"He left the message almost an hour ago. Try calling him back."

Jo quickly dialed his number. The call went directly to voice mail. "He's not answering."

"I wonder what's going on," Delta muttered.

"There's only one way to find out."

Jo silently wondered if perhaps all of the changes – the upcoming wedding, the renovations to his home and now a body being found were more than Gary could comfortably handle.

She loved Delta, bless her heart, but the woman's personality was a force to be reckoned with.

Gary, however, was quiet and low-key. Delta and Gary were the perfect example of opposites attracting. Perhaps he was getting cold feet, not only because he didn't want to burden the others with his current problem, but because he was genuinely having second thoughts.

Thankfully, it was a quick trip to Gary's place. They turned onto the long and winding driveway. Jo circled around and parked alongside the farm's pickup. She shut the engine off and reached for the door handle.

Delta stared out the front windshield but didn't make a move.

"Aren't you getting out?"

"Look." Delta jabbed her finger toward the corner of the house.

Jo followed her gaze, her stomach churning when she realized what Delta was pointing at.

Chapter 11

A Smith County investigator's van was parked near Gary's back door. A man walked past the front of Jo's vehicle. He placed a bag in the back of the van before returning inside.

"I see Nash." Jo made a beeline for the front porch with Delta hot on her heels. "What's going on?" she asked as soon as they reached Nash.

"The investigators showed up with a search warrant."

Jo lowered her voice. "Where's Gary?"

"Inside. I think he's in shock."

"I'll go check on him." Delta squeezed past them and made her way into the house. Moments later, they could hear Delta, her voice raised as she demanded to know what the authorities were searching for.

Another voice joined in. They grew louder, and Jo cringed. "Do you think we should referee?"

"Delta can handle herself."

"I'm not worried about Delta. I'm worried about the investigators." Jo followed the sound of the voices leading to a back bedroom. Her heart plummeted at what she saw. It looked as if someone had broken in and ransacked the place.

Picture frames were off kilter. A black floor safe was in the corner, its door wide open, and the contents spilled onto the floor.

"And another thing." Delta wagged her finger. "Tearing through a man's belongings is unacceptable. It looks like a wild animal got loose in here."

A youngish man with brown glasses cowered in the corner while another investigator slipped out of the room.

"I bet you wouldn't treat your parents' property in such a manner, young man," she scolded.

"I…we'll clean it up. We're almost done."

"I should hope so." Delta threw her hands in the air. "I'm scared to think what the rest of this place looks like."

"You might not want to go into the main bedroom."

Jo almost felt sorry for the man. Although Delta did have a point, there was no sense in trashing Gary's house.

Jo and Nash left Delta to supervise the cleanup of Gary's bedroom office. They headed to the kitchen, where they found him seated at the kitchen table, his head in his hands. Not wanting to scare him, Jo cleared her throat as she approached. "Hey, Gary," she said softly.

"Huh?" His head shot up, a dazed expression on his face. "Oh. Hi, Jo."

She placed a light hand on his shoulder. "The investigators promised to clean the place up."

"It doesn't matter. It needed a good cleaning anyway."

Nash pulled out a chair. "We saw them carry a bag from the house. Do you know what was in it?"

Gary stared blankly; as if unable to comprehend the question. "They took something from the house?"

"A bag," Jo repeated. "We watched them put it in their van."

"I dunno. I've been sitting here the whole time." Jo's heart went out to the poor man. He looked hopeless, or maybe it was resigned. She lifted her eyes, casting Nash a concerned look.

"I'm sure this is standard procedure," Nash said. "They'll be out of here in no time and close this case."

Sheriff Franklin appeared in the doorway. "Hey, Gary. I...uh. I got a complaint from one of the investigators. He said he's being harassed."

Delta's voice echoed from the back. "...not over there. Am I gonna have to take care of it myself?"

Franklin briefly closed his eyes. "Delta's here?"

"She's supervising the cleanup," Jo said. "She's not happy with the way they're tearing Gary's place apart, which I might add will soon be her home."

"This explains a lot." The sheriff tipped his hat. "I'll go back there and see what I can do to help."

"Good luck." Jo braced herself for more loud voices. Instead, it grew eerily quiet. She wasn't sure which was worse.

A red-faced Delta hustled into the kitchen moments later, her eyes zeroing in on Gary. "There you are." She bustled across the room. "Don't you worry. Those fellas are going to have this place shipshape in no time."

"It doesn't matter." Gary sucked in a breath. "I can see the writing on the wall. They're going to find some sort of evidence tying me to Barnaby's

157

death and lock me up. I'll never see the light of day again."

"Bite your tongue," Delta snapped. "No such thing is going to happen. You didn't kill Iteen. It's only a matter of time before they figure out who did."

Gary's hand trembled as he patted his shirt. "I forgot my jacket at the farm. Nash and I were in such a hurry that I left without it. It's in the garden shed."

"I'll grab it when I get home," Jo promised.

"No, I'll go get it." Gary pushed his chair back.

The sheriff appeared in the doorway. "Hey, Gary. The guys are almost done. I have a quick question for you."

Gary's expression changed in an instant, from looking defeated to enraged as he turned his wrath on the sheriff. "I've about reached my limit. My house is a wreck. You and your boys better hurry up before I throw you out of here."

Jo's heart skipped a beat as Gary advanced on him.

"Now, Gary. Like I said, we're almost done." The sheriff placed a light hand on his holster. "There's no reason to get riled up."

"Jo and I will go get your jacket and bring it back." Nash grasped Jo's elbow and propelled her toward the door.

"I'll stay here to keep an eye on things." Delta stumbled back as her betrothed brushed past her, a dark look on his face as he followed the sheriff.

Jo rushed to her friend's side. "Are you sure you want to stay? Things are getting a little tense."

"I can handle myself."

"We'll make it quick." Jo hurried behind Nash as he strode out of the house and climbed into her SUV. She waited until they were on the road to talk. "Gary's a wreck."

"You should've seen the look on his face when the cops showed up at the farm."

"You don't think..." Jo let the unfinished question hang in the air. She didn't dare speak what the small voice in the back of her head was suggesting.

"That Gary could actually be responsible for Barnaby's death?" Nash rubbed a weary hand across his brow. "Gary's a good guy, one of the best."

"But even good people can do bad things when provoked. You saw how angry he got right before we left."

"I did, and to be honest, I've never seen him lose his temper before. His dad had a reputation for being a hothead. In fact, Gary's mentioned a time or two in passing how, when he was growing up, his dad didn't spare the rod when he felt one of his children had done wrong."

"So, there's a chance that hot-headedness was passed on." An uneasiness filled Jo. She loved Gary. He was like family, but in all honesty, she didn't know him well.

Not long after Jo moved to Divine, he'd shown up on her doorstep, offering his assistance. They chatted often but mostly about the farm. In fact, the more she thought about it, the more she realized she knew very little about him.

But Delta knew him. If she'd had any misgivings about Gary, surely she would've confided in Jo. Unless she was so eager to get married that she overlooked some warning signs.

Jo thought about their visit to Centerpoint earlier and their encounter with Charlie Golden. "Have you ever heard the name Charlie Golden?"

"Yeah. They call him Crazy Charlie. He's a nice enough guy. He's been taking care of the chapel and grounds for years now."

"Delta and I were there earlier today." Jo briefly told him about their visit to Half Wall Bar and Sonny Pabst suggesting they visit Charlie.

Nash eyed her with surprise. "You went to the bar?"

"To do a little digging around. We met the owner, Florence Parlow. She was reluctant to discuss Barnaby's death, but Sonny Pabst, one of her regulars, wasn't."

"Florence has had some rough goings-on over at that bar, although I wouldn't know of it firsthand."

Jo's cell phone chimed. "It's Delta." She pressed the answer button. "Hey, Delta."

"Hey, Jo. You home yet?"

"Close. We're right around the corner."

Delta said something in a low voice, something Jo couldn't make out. "Can you repeat what you said?"

"Hang on." There was some tapping on the other end of the line. "Gary's gone ballistic. It happened as soon as the investigators asked to take a look in his cellar."

"The cellar?"

"I think there's something down there," Delta whispered. "In fact, I've never been in his cellar. What if there are more bodies stashed down there?"

"Delta," Jo chided. "Do you seriously suspect Gary has been hiding bodies?"

"I'm beginning to wonder. He's becoming unhinged. Are you coming back?"

"Yes, with his jacket. We'll hurry." Jo told her to stay safe and then set her phone in the center console. She repeated what Delta had told her.

Back at the farm, the couple headed to the garden shed, which was Gary's domain. Everything had a place, and Gary was particular about it. This could be one of the reasons why he was freaking out about the investigators tearing his home apart.

The couple searched the shed. The jacket was nowhere to be found. "It's not here."

"Maybe he left it in the workshop and forgot," Nash said. "We were in there talking when the cops showed up."

They made their way to the workshop. The lights were on, and the faint aroma of fresh sawdust filled the air.

They searched the workshop and then the small office. There was still no sign of Gary's jacket; or any jacket, for that matter.

"Maybe he left it in his truck." Jo reached for her phone and tapped out a message to Delta, asking her to check.

She replied moments later. "No jacket. Crud." Jo rubbed her palms together. "The jacket couldn't have sprouted legs and walked off."

"What about Leah? Maybe she's seen his jacket."

"Good idea." They hustled out of the workshop and made their way around the side of the barn, past the smaller of the two gardens. "She's not here."

"What about the chicken coop?" Nash asked.

"You're right. Let's check the coop."

The couple circled back and found Leah standing near the door. She did a double-take when she saw them. "How's Gary?"

"He's still at his place with the police," Jo said.

Leah's eyes grew round as saucers.

"We're looking for Gary's jacket. He said he left it in the garden shed."

"He did." Leah set the wicker basket she was holding on top of the coop. "I put it inside the cabinet after he left. He's very particular about keeping his jacket with him." She explained that she'd put it away when she realized he'd forgotten it.

Nash thanked her for the heads up, and then he and Jo returned to the shed. "I'll run in and grab it."

Jo waited for him near the door. When he emerged, he was holding a tan windbreaker. "Oh good. You found it."

"I did." There was an odd expression on Nash's face.

"What's wrong?"

"When I grabbed the jacket, this fell out."

Chapter 12

"Benzodiazepine. Warning: May cause drowsiness, dizziness, agitation and memory loss." Jo's eyes squinted as she peered at the prescription bottle in Nash's hand. "What is this?"

"It's an anti-anxiety medication. My ex was on these. In fact, she became addicted to them."

"Gary is taking anxiety medicine? I wonder if Delta knows." Jo sucked in a breath. "No wonder he was so anxious to track down his jacket. I say we keep quiet about finding this."

"I was thinking the same thing. It's none of our business." Nash placed the bottle of pills back inside the jacket pocket. "I'll run back there to drop this off unless you want to ride along."

"You go on ahead. I have some things to take care of around here. Besides, I'm sure the residents are wondering what's going on." After Nash left, Jo made her way to the mercantile.

She checked in with Kelli and Raylene first and then ran next door to the bakeshop. Jo waited until Michelle and Laverne, who were helping customers, were free before approaching the counter. "How's it going?"

"We've already sold out of Delta's blueberry pies," Michelle said.

"How's Gary?" Laverne asked. "We saw him and Nash leaving with the cops."

Jo gave Laverne a pointed stare. "My reason for stopping by here is to remind everyone that Gary's current situation is none of our business and nothing we should be discussing."

"I was just asking." Laverne lifted a brow. "It doesn't look good for the cops to be here when customers arrive."

"I don't disagree, but I believe the less we talk about it – or gossip – the better." Jo wandered over to the advertisement for Miles' theater's grand opening. "Have any customers commented about the grand opening?"

"Yep," Michelle said. "I've been mentioning it to everyone who comes in. Thanks for dropping Sherry off for a visit earlier."

"I'm glad she was free and took the time to see everyone."

"She stayed for a while, and then Nash gave her a ride home. That was before..."

"Before the police arrived," Jo guessed.

"Yeah."

"I've invited her to dinner, so hopefully, she'll be back again soon." Jo had started to go when Laverne stopped her. "I noticed Delta hasn't come back yet."

"No, she hasn't."

"I was wondering if you needed any help in the kitchen."

"Are you trying to get your foot in Delta's kitchen while she's not around?"

"Me?" Laverne feigned innocence as she pressed a hand to her chest. "Here I am, trying to do something nice, and you're questioning my motives."

A tinge of guilt filled Jo. Perhaps Laverne's motives were innocent. She contemplated the woman's offer. Not only did Jo have no clue what to make for dinner, hanging out with Laverne would give her a chance to have a one on one chat with the new resident and get her take on how things were going. "I suppose, but just this once."

Although Jo relented, she still wasn't convinced there wasn't an ulterior motive behind Laverne's request. "I'll meet you in the kitchen unless Michelle needs you."

"I should be fine working by myself. Our mornings are busier than the afternoons."

"Great." Laverne hurried out of the store.

"Hey!" Jo ran after her. "Where's the fire?"

"I didn't want to wait around for you to change your mind."

"You know how Delta feels about her kitchen."

Laverne rolled her eyes. "The kitchen is Delta's domain. We can only be in her hallowed halls if we're graced with a royal invitation."

"Very funny." Jo gave her a playful nudge.

"I have to swap out my clothes for more appropriate kitchen attire. I'll see you in a few." Laverne arrived minutes later, sporting an apron with a catchphrase on the front.

Jo grinned. "I like your apron. Lead me to the cook's nook."

"Thanks. It was a gift from one of the prison cooks." Laverne rubbed her palms together. "So, what's the meal plan?"

"I don't have one. Since this is more your field of expertise than mine, I thought you could take a look around and come up with an idea. Nothing too fancy," Jo warned.

"I'm on it." Laverne made a beeline for the well-stocked pantry. There was enough food on hand to feed a small army for a month. Delta's motto was better to be prepared than to suffer without.

Laverne began humming as she stepped inside. There was some banging around, and she emerged moments later, a can of black beans in hand. "How do you feel about spicy dishes?"

"It depends on what kind of spicy."

"The best kind – Mexican."

Jo patted her stomach. "I love Mexican, and so do the others."

"Great. I have the perfect dish." Laverne began gathering the ingredients moving from the pantry to the counter.

"Let me help." Jo worked alongside her, assembling the ingredients. "What are we making?"

"Laverne's Lucky 7-Layer Burritos." She explained that, while the recipe was designed to be a dip, it also worked great for burritos. "My cellmate, Christina, gave me this recipe. This is the real deal."

"You have it memorized?"

"It's all right here." Laverne tapped the side of her forehead. "There's some chopping involved, but the rest is easy breezy."

Jo set a cutting board on the counter. "You seem to be settling in here on the farm."

"Yeah. The other residents have been cool. They're nicer than some of the staff at the prison."

"We have a great bunch of women living here."

Laverne reached for the can opener. "You still have an open spot."

"I've decided to wait until after the wedding to fill the opening."

"And you get your suggestions from Pastor Murphy."

"Most of the time. That's how I found you." Jo remembered her initial meeting with Laverne and then her second. Both times, she was sure the woman was a no-go. An unanticipated dilemma forced Jo to change her mind. Looking back, she was convinced God had intervened.

"I was thinking. I mean, I know it's not my place to state my opinion."

"Which has never stopped you before," Jo interrupted.

"True. Not to mention I'm the low woman on the totem pole, but I might have someone in mind. Christina, my former cellmate." Laverne hurried on. "She should be up for some sort of sainthood. I mean, she put up with me. Anyway, I think she would be a perfect candidate for this place. She's getting out soon."

Jo began rinsing the tomatoes. "I've never had a resident make a recommendation. If she's up for consideration when I'm ready to fill the spot, I'm sure she'll be on the list."

"It was just a thought."

Jo spied Delta's recipe holder on the counter. "I think I found Delta's dinner plan."

"What is...was it?"

"Stuffed peppers and..." Jo removed the recipe and glanced at the one beneath it. "Grilled corn and red cabbage slaw."

"Gross." Laverne made a gagging sound. "I hate peppers. They're disgusting. Even the thought of touching one makes me want to vomit."

"Seriously?"

"It involves a meal my mom made for my school lunch. She was big on fruits and vegetables – and all into the whole food pyramid thing. Anyhoo, she loved peppers, but they literally made me physically ill."

"You don't say." Jo arched a brow.

"I lost my cookies right there at the cafeteria lunch table. It was either the pepper or the pickled bologna she made me eat." Laverne opened the cans of beans and dumped them in a saucepan. "It left a lasting impression."

"I'm sorry to hear that."

While they worked, they chatted about life on the farm. Laverne insisted that she didn't have any complaints or concerns and even thanked Jo again for the fragrance-free body soaps and laundry detergent.

When Jo asked her about her psychiatric background, she really lit up, rambling on about her interest in mental health and chemical imbalances.

The conversation reminded Jo of what Nash had found in Gary's jacket pocket. "How much do you know about Benzodiazepine?"

Laverne's head whipped around. "If you're not careful, Benzodiazepine can be bad news. It's highly addictive. I hope you're not on that stuff."

"I'm not."

"Is someone you know?" Laverne pressed.

"I'm not at liberty to answer your question."

"I've never taken it myself, but if you do, be very careful." Laverne rattled off some of the drug's side effects, which were similar to what Nash had already told her, not to mention what she'd read on the warning label.

Raylene arrived a short time later, offering to help. The conversation about the drug was forgotten as Jo worked hard to get dinner on the table, making her appreciate Delta even more.

The platters of burritos made their rounds, with everyone complimenting Laverne on the delicious dish. She shot Jo a triumphant look, and she could almost see the woman's wheels turning as she plotted her kitchen takeover.

During the meal, they discussed the movie and dinner theater's grand opening. Jo was careful not to mention Sherry's VIP invitation. The others would find out soon enough, although Jo suspected Raylene already knew since she and Sherry were close.

The meal ended, and the women pitched in to clean up. While they worked, Nash pulled Jo aside. "I gave Gary his jacket, but I didn't mention what we found in the pocket."

"Good. Since Gary's doctor prescribed it, I think it's best for us to leave well enough alone."

"Agreed," Nash said.

"What about Delta?"

"She was surprisingly calm and subdued. I think she's trying to do whatever she can to help Gary." Nash waited until Kelli passed by to continue the conversation. "I'm going to have to skip tonight's swing date. I didn't get much done work-wise today, and I have a mess out in the workshop to clean up."

"I'll give you a pass this time," Jo teased. "Don't let it happen again."

"Yes, ma'am." Nash snapped to attention and gave her a mock salute before leaning in and sneaking a quick kiss. "I'll see you in the morning."

"Bright and early." Jo made her way into the kitchen only to discover the residents had already finished cleaning up.

The others left. Raylene lingered behind, waiting until she and Jo were alone. "Are Delta and Gary okay?"

"I hope so. It's been a long day for them."

"Thanks for dropping Sherry off earlier. It was nice to see her."

"She needs to come by more often." Jo shifted her feet. "I'm thrilled she's doing well and adjusting to life on her own."

"More than adjusting," Raylene said. "I heard Miles invited her to his VIP box for the theater's grand opening."

"He did. I hope…" Jo paused, carefully choosing her words. "I hope it all works out."

"I know what you mean. Me too." Raylene turned to go and then turned back. "I'll see you tomorrow morning."

"Yes, for breakfast and then to wait for your visitor's arrival."

A flicker of doubt flitted across Raylene's face. "Do you think I made a mistake in agreeing to meet with Brock's brother?"

Jo considered the question. "No. Because you would always wonder what he wanted, that perhaps there was a chance to finally have some closure over what happened that tragic night all those years ago."

"I can't help but think there's another reason for his visit besides shutting down the business. Why would he make a trip halfway across the country to meet with the person he believes was responsible for his brother's death?"

"There's only one way to find out." Jo offered her an encouraging smile. "We'll get through it."

"Thanks for the pep talk." Raylene stopped when she reached the bottom step. "I almost forgot. The women and I were watching the local news before we came over for dinner. The forecasters are predicting rough weather tomorrow. There's potential for some bad storms moving through."

Jo immediately thought about what Charlie Golden had told them. "I'll check the forecast. Thanks for the heads up."

"You're welcome."

After she left, Jo and Duke headed out for an evening walk around the farm. A stiff northerly wind had picked up, whipping around the side of the house. She shifted her gaze to Nash's workshop, where the lights burned brightly.

Jo and the pup stopped by the mailbox to collect the mail and then inspected the porch's hanging baskets. It had been the perfect growing season not only for the flowers but for the vegetable gardens and fruit trees.

As she wandered around, Jo thought about Gary and Delta, about Raylene's upcoming visit. She prayed for God's hand on not only them but all of the residents as well.

She made a mental note to stop by Miles' theater to offer her help. She also wanted to chat with Marlee to get her take not only on Flo Parlow but to find out if she'd heard anything new about Barnaby Iteen.

They finished their inspection and walk, but Delta still hadn't returned, so once Jo had settled on the porch swing, she sent a text to make sure Delta was okay. With a quick glance at her watch, she knew the deli had closed for the evening. She dialed Marlee's number and left a message.

She was still on the porch when Marlee returned the call. "Hey, Jo. You must've read my mind. How are Delta and Gary?"

"The investigators showed up today with a warrant to search Gary's place. Delta hasn't come back yet, so I don't know what's going on."

"I have a connection," Marlee said. "Let me do a little digging around tonight. I might be able to get more info than what's being released to the public."

"Anything you can find out is appreciated," Jo said. "I'm going to stop by Miles' theater in the morning and thought I would swing by the deli sometime after nine if that works for you."

"I'll be here. I should have heard something by then."

While talking with Marlee, Delta had texted back, saying she was okay and would be home later, but not to wait up for her.

Knowing there was most likely a long day ahead, Jo decided to turn in early. She plugged her cell phone in the charger and climbed into bed. She had just drifted off to sleep when the phone chirped.

Thinking it was Delta, she bolted upright and turned her light on. It was an alert from the National Weather Service. "Severe weather warning alert..." The message displayed was a warning for potentially dangerous weather within the next twenty-four hours.

Jo grabbed her television's remote control and flipped through the channels until reaching the national weather channel. It took a few minutes for the forecasters to report on their area.

She got goosebumps when the meteorologist warned of the potential for a "finger of God" event. "With this cool mass steamrolling down from Canada and a warm air mass speeding up from the Gulf, we have the potential for some extremely strong storms, starting tomorrow afternoon." The meteorologist advised people in the cone of concern to stay tuned for updates.

The report ended, and Jo switched the television off. She prayed for safety for all of the residents and for the town of Divine. As she drifted off to sleep, an uneasy feeling settled over her as she remembered Charlie Golden's words. He had told her and Delta that supercell storms were on the way.

If what the forecasters and Charlie said was true, tomorrow was shaping up to be one wild roller coaster ride.

Little did Joanna Pepperdine know how wild the ride would be.

Chapter 13

Jo stood near the back of the garden shed, searching for a watering can. "Now, where can it be?" she muttered under her breath as she began digging through the bins.

The shed door rattled. Jo spun around. "Who's there?"

The doorway was empty. "Must be the wind," Jo muttered under her breath as she resumed her search.

The door rattled again, this time louder, causing the hair on her arms to stand straight up. She stumbled back. "Who's there?"

Whack!

Without warning, the door was ripped from its hinges. It became airborne and then spun like a top. Around and around, it twirled.

A gust of icy air flooded the shed. Drawn to the now open doorway, she fearfully lifted her eyes skyward. It had turned ominously dark, almost black.

"Joanna." A familiar figure appeared in the doorway.

Jo swallowed hard. "Dad," she whispered.

"A storm is coming. You're not safe here." A roaring sound filled the air, drowning out his voice.

"I can't hear you!" Jo shielded her face as dirt and debris flew through the air. "Dad!"

The roaring grew louder. A dark cloud dipped down, forming a funnel as it danced across the open field, mere feet from the farm. Jo tried to lift her arm, to warn her father what was behind him.

The twirling storm was bearing down on them, picking up speed and growing larger by the second.

"A tornado." Jo willed her feet to move, but they were cemented to the ground. "Daaaaad." She could feel the storm pulling her, sucking her into its vortex. A chunk of wood flew through the air, hitting her in the head. A sharp pain pierced her skull.

Jo shot upright in bed, taking short breaths as she struggled to get her bearings. "My bedroom," she gasped. "I'm in my room."

Tick. Tock.

Tick. Tock. The tick-tock of her wall clock was the only sound.

"It was a dream." She closed her eyes and sucked in a breath. "It was only a dream."

Duke padded across the floor.

Jo's hand trembled as she reached out to pat his head. The remnants of the dream played over again. Her father. He was there.

Duke nudged her hand with his snout. It wasn't the first time her pup had comforted her after a bad dream. Although this was the first time in a long time that she'd dreamt about her father.

Jo switched her bedside lamp on and reached for her Bible. She turned to the familiar marker and began reading Psalm 91:

He that dwelleth in the secret place of the most High shall abide under the shadow of the Almighty. I will say of the Lord, He is my refuge and my fortress: my God; in him will I trust.

Surely he shall deliver thee from the snare of the fowler, and from the noisome pestilence. He shall cover thee with his feathers, and under his wings shalt thou trust: his truth shall be thy shield and buckler.

Thou shalt not be afraid for the terror by night; nor for the arrow that flieth by day; Nor for the pestilence that walketh in darkness; nor for the destruction that wasteth at noonday. A thousand shall fall at thy side, and ten thousand at thy right hand; but it shall not come nigh thee.

Jo read it twice and then pressed the Bible to her chest as she prayed for peace. Not only for herself, but for Nash, for Gary and Delta, for Raylene and the other residents as well.

It took a long time for Jo to fall back asleep. The next morning, flashbacks of the dream lingered as she showered and dressed.

Delta was already in the kitchen when Jo arrived. "You look like you put in a rough night."

"I did." Jo poured a cup of coffee and watched Delta work. "I had a bad dream."

"About your mother?" Delta stopped what she was doing, a look of concern on her face.

"It was my father this time." Jo sipped her coffee as she remembered every detail, from her hair standing on end to her feet being cemented to the ground. "I was in the garden shed. A big storm was coming, and my father was standing there, trying to warn me." Jo's voice cracked, and her eyes started to burn. "The tornado was coming for him. I couldn't help him. I couldn't move. All I could do was watch."

"Oh, dear." Delta wiped her hands on her apron and hurried over. "I'm sorry, Jo. It was a rough day yesterday, and I feel partly to blame."

Jo dabbed at the tears in her eyes. "It's not your fault. I...it kind of goes with the territory."

"Well, Gary and me, we're gonna be fine. Don't you worry about us. Those investigators aren't going to find anything in the stuff they took. Heck, they probably did us a favor. Gary's a packrat." Delta waved dismissively. "In fact, I told one of them before he left that he could keep it."

Jo's sadness was momentarily forgotten at the thought of Delta telling the investigators to keep the stuff. "I bet they didn't know what to think."

"Honey, they got out of there as fast as they could." Delta returned to the counter. "I'm sorry I wasn't here to make dinner. How did it go?"

"We missed you and Gary. Laverne gave me a hand in the kitchen and whipped up a delicious seven-layer burrito."

"I heard."

"There are leftovers in the fridge." Jo filled her in on the day's schedule, how Aaron Beck was arriving at nine to meet with Raylene. "After that, I'm heading to town to see what Marlee knows and to check in on Miles."

Delta finished whisking the muffin batter and poured it into the greased muffin tins. "Do you want me to tag along?"

"I appreciate the offer, but I'm sure you have things you want to catch up on around here." Jo refilled their coffee cups and spied something sitting on the counter. "What's this?"

"Laverne left me a note."

Jo read it aloud. "Hey, Delta. Your kitchen is super sweet. Lucky dog. I helped with dinner, and there are leftovers in the fridge. We found your recipes. I'm sure your stuffed peppers are delicious as far as peppers are concerned. The burritos were a big hit. I would love to serve them at your wedding." Jo chuckled. "Laverne doesn't like peppers."

"I figured as much." Delta carried the muffin tins to the oven. "I take everything that comes out of Laverne's mouth with a grain of salt."

"Or maybe even, two. I need to take care of a few things." Jo placed the note back on the counter before heading to her office to get ready for Aaron's arrival.

She cleared her desk first, careful to remove any confidential information regarding her residents. After finishing, she checked her emails. There was one from Pastor Murphy with a subject line, "Potential Residents."

Jo clicked on the link and carefully went through the list he'd attached. There were six in all. The one near the bottom caught Jo's eye. "Christina Lopez."

She briefly wondered if this was the woman Laverne had mentioned.

She studied the potential residents' profiles and then jotted some notes along with questions for Pastor Murphy. As was her habit, she printed each of the attachments and then sorted them, placing the most promising one on top.

Christina was near the middle at number four. Jo's main concern over the woman was her background and the notation that she was considered to be a flight risk since she had close family ties in Mexico.

Jo had just finished sending a reply to the pastor when she heard a light rap on her door. Raylene appeared. "Hey, Jo."

"Good morning." Jo motioned her inside. "Are you ready for today?"

"Yes. I want to get it over with." Raylene nervously tugged the bottom of her blouse. "He didn't happen to change his mind, did he?"

Jo checked her cell phone. "No. I don't have any messages."

Raylene pressed a light hand to her stomach. "I barely slept last night."

"It will be all right," Jo's voice softened. "The meeting will be over before you know it."

"Right. I'll go see if Delta needs a hand."

After Raylene left, Jo stared out the window. With God, anything was possible, even forgiveness, in what appeared to be hopeless situations. She had to admit, it was a long way to travel just to tell someone you forgave them. A nagging thought that perhaps there was something else hovered in the back of Jo's mind.

She remembered the time she'd encouraged Sherry to reach out to her family and how it had backfired. They wanted nothing to do with her. In fact, her father had told her not to contact them ever again.

Not long after, Sherry had decided to make Divine her permanent home. Although Jo was saddened by the family's rejection, she was thrilled to have her former resident nearby. And, by all accounts, Sherry was doing wonderfully.

The tantalizing aroma of bacon frying lured Jo from her office. She joined the others in the kitchen and began carrying the platters of food to the table.

"Storms are brewing," Leah reported as soon as the group finished praying. "The chickens told me."

Laverne snorted. "What did they say? Cackle, cackle, storms are on the horizon."

"No. There are other signs. It would be easier to show you."

Gary, who had joined them, chimed in. "Leah is right. Farm animals are excellent weather forecasters."

There was some discussion on the hens' reactions, with both Gary and Leah insisting the animals knew.

"I got a weather warning on my phone last night. The hens are right. There are storms brewing. They aren't hitting until later this afternoon," Jo said.

Michelle's eyes grew round as saucers. "Bad storms?"

"They called them supercells. I'm hoping the forecasts are accurate, and they hold off until later today," Jo said. "I have some errands to run this morning."

After the meal ended, everyone followed Leah and Gary out to the chicken coop. Jo heard them before they even rounded the side of the barn. Both hens were making a terrible racket.

They gathered around the coop, watching as the hens skittered back and forth, their feathers ruffled. At one point, they collided, causing an even louder ruckus.

"Which is which?" Jo asked.

Leah pointed to the hen near the watering dish. "This one is Henrietta. The one on the ramp is Egglina."

"They're as nervous as a chicken in a fox's den," Gary said.

Leah clasped her hands, nervously eyeing the sky. "What will we do with them? I don't want them left outdoors if bad storms are coming."

"We can put them in the barn." Gary explained that he'd built the coop so the top half could be removed, creating a makeshift carrying cage. "We'll do it right after lunch."

"The clouds are moving fast." Nash removed his cell phone from his pocket and tapped the top. "Tornado watches are extending out in a hundred-mile radius."

"I'm gonna straighten up the cellar," Gary said. "We might need to head down there if things get too bad."

While the group discussed the imminent storms, Laverne crept past them, tiptoeing along the side of the coop. One of the hens immediately stopped clucking and barreled toward her. She wrapped her claws around the wire meshing, straining in vain to poke her beak through the opening as she made a screeching sound.

"Henrietta is wound up," Nash said.

As Laverne inched along the front, the bird kept pace, all the while screeching and poking her beak through the poultry netting. "That nasty bird is trying to get me again."

"Henrietta is the one who attacked Laverne yesterday." Leah placed a light hand on the fence not far from the hen and cooed softly. The hen cocked her head, listening as Leah cooed again.

Henrietta hopped down. Cool as a cucumber, she sauntered off, pecking the coop's floor.

Laverne's jaw dropped. "How did you do that?"

"Henrietta is nervous about the weather. The cooing calms them."

"Thank you for the lesson in bird language." Jo patted her arm. "You do have a magic touch with the animals. It's shaping up to be a busy day and time to get to work."

The residents headed off in different directions. Gary and Leah began making their way to the back to check on the gardens.

It was Michelle's turn to work with Nash, and he decided their first task was to make their rounds, checking for any items needing to be secured in anticipation of the severe weather.

Delta hurried off to begin gathering candles, flashlights and other supplies while Jo and Raylene trailed behind, making their way toward the house just before nine. They made it as far as the front porch when the sound of tires on gravel caught their attention.

The women paused at the top of the steps, watching as a four-door sedan circled the drive and parked near the porch. A man, in his early forties, if Jo had to guess, climbed out of the vehicle and made his way toward them.

"It's him," Raylene whispered in a low voice.

Jo gave a small nod and then approached the top step to greet Raylene's visitor.

Chapter 14

Jo wasn't sure what she envisioned Aaron Beck to look like, but she wasn't expecting him to look so young. And handsome with wavy dark locks that curled up around his neck. He sported a five o'clock shadow, and as he drew closer, his sultry eyes were almost mesmerizing.

"Good morning." The man made his way around the car, slowing when Raylene stepped next to Jo. "Hello, Raylene."

Jo could hear a faint tremor in Raylene's voice as she greeted him. "Hello, Aaron. You're right on time."

"I…didn't want to keep you waiting. I wasn't sure how long the drive would take from Kansas City."

Jo made her way down the steps and extended a hand. "I'm Joanna Pepperdine, the owner of this farm."

"Aaron Beck. Thank you for allowing me to visit on such short notice." His grip was firm, warm...confident.

Their eyes met, and Jo immediately got a good feeling about him. He wasn't here to cause trouble for Raylene. She could feel it in her bones. "It's a long drive. Please, come in."

Raylene stepped back as Jo led their visitor into the house. "Can I get you a cup of coffee? Some water?"

"No, thanks. I won't be staying long."

"Then, I'll show you where you and Raylene can have a private word." They entered the hall leading past the half bath to Jo's office at the end. She stepped aside to give him room as Raylene followed behind.

She gave her resident a small smile, hoping her look conveyed everything was going to be all right. "Raylene has asked me to sit in on your visit...meeting if that's all right."

"Yes, ma'am." Aaron took a seat near the window, his eyes on Raylene as she perched on the edge of the chair, semi-facing him. "As I said in my letter, I asked one of Brock's friends to track you down. I meant to do it last year after I heard you were released from prison." An awkward silence ensued as he faltered. He lowered his head and stared down at his hands.

"Raylene has been living here since her release," Jo explained.

"Your farm – your home is a halfway house for former convicts."

"It is."

"I've been rehearsing what I was going to say all the way here." Aaron shifted uncomfortably. "The fact of the matter is I want to apologize for the awful things I said about you during your trial, Raylene."

He continued. "I was angry, angry at the world, angry at you, angry at Brock for getting involved in that case. After he was...gone, you were the only one left to take my anger out on, and I'm sorry."

Raylene sat motionless, staring at Aaron as a lone tear trickled down her cheek.

Jo placed her hand on the woman's shoulder and gave it a gentle squeeze.

His voice was raw when he spoke again. "I hope you'll find it in your heart to forgive me. I know you didn't kill Brock. You loved him."

"I did," Raylene whispered. "His death haunts me every day."

"Brock wouldn't want you to blame yourself. It was an accident. It took me years to face the fact. I reviewed every file, every witness account, every report. You were unfairly convicted. I feel partly to blame because I think the family impact statement sealed your fate."

Jo's throat constricted as she watched Raylene grasp Aaron's hand. "Thank you for believing me and apologizing. You don't..." She sucked in a ragged breath, and Jo could feel her pain, feel the emotion. "...know how much this means to me."

Aaron reached into his pocket, pulled out an envelope, and handed it to Raylene. "These are notes from the family. Mom and Dad and my siblings asked me to give these to you."

Raylene's hand trembled as she took the envelope. She stared at it for a long time before placing it on the edge of the desk. "I'll read them. Maybe not today, but soon," she promised.

"That's all I can ask." Aaron slowly stood. "I should get going."

"Why don't you stay a little longer," Jo said gently. "Perhaps Raylene can show you around."

"I..." Aaron shot Raylene a questioning look.

"Yes. That's a great idea, Jo." Raylene swiped at her eyes, and Jo was sure she was doing everything in her power to keep from breaking down.

"While you're gone, I'll make some iced tea, and you can sample some of the most amazing, sweet treats this side of the Mississippi River when you return."

Aaron offered Jo a grateful look before slowly rising to his feet. "I accept your gracious invitation."

Jo hung back, waiting for Raylene and her visitor to exit the office before following them as far as the front door.

"I've done some research on this place," Aaron said. "You run an impressive operation."

"Thank you. It's a labor of love."

"Jo does an amazing job of keeping everything running smoothly. I swear she's part angel." Raylene and Aaron stepped out of the house as Jo lingered near the door, watching them as they began making their way to the barn. "Thank you, God."

Her heart nearly burst as Raylene's demeanor relaxed. She shoved her hands in her back pockets as she casually strolled alongside Aaron.

Jo quietly closed the front door and wandered into the kitchen, where she found Delta standing at the counter testing the flashlights. "I see Raylene's visitor showed up. How did it go?"

Jo gave her a thumbs up. "Better than expected. Aaron asked Raylene to forgive him. He brought letters from the family."

"Thank you, Jesus." Delta let out a joyful whoop. "Finally, some good news."

"Very good news. Raylene is showing him around, and then he's going to have tea. I promised him one of your amazing goodies before he heads out."

"Well, then I'm gonna send him off in grand style." Delta dropped the flashlight and bustled to the baked goods tray she kept on hand for residents and anyone else who happened to drop by.

She grabbed the tiered tray and carried it to the table. "I'm sure there's something in here that will tempt Aaron's sweet tooth."

"Without a doubt." Jo did a quick check of the clock. Even if he stayed for an hour, she would still have plenty of time to head into town for a quick chat with Marlee and to check in with Miles.

Delta shifted the tray and took a step back, eyeing it critically. "Are you still planning on heading into town this morning?"

"I am. Since we took Raylene off this morning's schedule because of her visitor, I might ask her if she wants to tag along."

"You know she's gonna say yes. I'm sure she would love to see Sherry for a few minutes to fill her in on what happened."

The front door slammed, and the tinkle of a woman's laughter echoed from the front of the house. A much more relaxed Raylene and Aaron appeared in the doorway.

"Aaron, I would like you to meet the best cook and baker extraordinaire, Delta Childress."

Delta hustled across the room and held out her hand. "My, my, aren't you the handsomest man I've laid eyes on in decades, Aaron Beck. It's my pleasure," she drawled. "Jo said she invited you to stay for a few minutes to enjoy some Divine hospitality."

"Yes, ma'am." Aaron politely nodded. "I hope I'm not inconveniencing you."

"Not at all. We love company. Have a seat."

The group gathered at the table as Jo furtively studied Raylene and Aaron's body language. It was like night and day from his initial arrival. Delta played the perfect hostess, easily keeping the conversation going as she plied Aaron with questions and goodies.

"I do appreciate your generosity and warm welcome." Aaron consulted his watch. "I should get going. I have an early afternoon flight out. I need to head home and get back to work."

"What line of work are you in, if you don't mind me asking," Jo said.

Raylene and Aaron exchanged a quick glance.

"I run a hunting and fishing business, but I'm considering following in my big brother's footsteps. I'm thinking about taking over Brock's business but doing some re-organizing to better suit my future plans. Since Raylene helped my brother start it, I figured I could ask her for some advice."

"And, from what you've told me, it should do quite well," Raylene added.

"I'm sure your brother is smiling down from heaven." Jo pushed her chair back and stood. "Thank you for making the trip here to visit Raylene."

"You should take some goodies with you." Delta sprang from her chair and darted to the counter. She grabbed a white bakery bag and began placing an array of treats inside. "You might want something to snack on later."

"Thank you," Aaron said as he took the bag. "Perhaps I'll see you again sometime."

"If you're ever out in this part of the country, by all means, please stop by." Jo, along with Raylene, escorted him back through the house and onto the porch.

Raylene stopped at the top of the steps. "Thanks again for coming all this way, Aaron."

"I'll get ahold of you again soon." He patted his pocket. "I have your email address."

"I would like that." Raylene gave him a small wave and joined Jo. They stood watching as he climbed into the car and drove out of sight. "I can't believe it."

"A big weight has been lifted off your shoulders."

"Bigger than you can imagine." Raylene briefly closed her eyes. "Miracles do happen."

"And to the nicest people." Jo changed the subject. "I'm heading to Marlee's deli for a quick chat. Since you're not on the work schedule this morning, would you like to tag along?"

"Yes. I can't wait to share my exciting news with Sherry."

Jo headed inside to grab her purse and keys and was waiting in the SUV when Raylene, who had gone back to her apartment, returned.

During the drive, Raylene chattered a mile a minute, about Aaron, about his family, her future plans and how she might start her own bounty hunting business with the money she had saved.

"Would you set down roots in the area?" Jo asked.

"Maybe. I don't know. I haven't thought that far ahead."

Since they were in between the breakfast and lunch hour, Jo easily found a parking spot in front of the deli. The women met on the sidewalk and then made their way inside.

Jo appreciatively sniffed as the tantalizing aroma of freshly baked bread filled the dining room. She caught a glimpse of Sherry, who was on the other side, waiting on a table as they walked to the back.

Marlee stood at the kitchen's center island, surrounded by mixing bowls and muffin tins. She did a double-take when they walked in. "Hey, Jo, Raylene. Sherry and I were just talking about you."

"Raylene." Sherry burst into the kitchen and gave her friend a warm hug. "I didn't know you were coming to town."

"Neither did I until a few minutes ago."

"We can't stay long," Jo warned. "We're going to stop by Miles' theater to check on him. I want to be home well ahead of the storms."

Marlee's expression sobered. "I was listening to the weather on my way in this morning. They're forecasting supercell storms for later today. I may close a little early if it looks like they're moving in."

"What about you, Sherry?" Jo asked. "Would you like to come out after your shift ends, just in case bad weather strikes?"

"I'm fine at the apartment." Sherry explained her landlord, Wayne Malton, who was also a friend of Jo's, had given her and Todd access to the basement. "We'll head down there if it looks like it's getting bad."

"You know you're always welcome."

"I do. Thank you."

"I want to show you something I picked up at the farmer's market the other day." Sherry led Raylene out of the kitchen.

Jo waited until they were gone. "I was wondering if you'd heard anything else about Barnaby Iteen's death."

"As a matter of fact, Evelyn McBride, one of the dispatchers for the Smith County Sheriff's Department, was in here earlier for breakfast. I cornered her to find out what she knows."

"And..." Jo prompted.

"I don't think you're going to like what I'm about to say."

Chapter 15

"They found a chunk of rope next to Iteen's body," Marlee said. "The investigators also found a pocket watch."

"I know about the watch," Jo said. "What does the rope have to do with the investigation?"

"They found the same type of rope in Gary's barn. Reading between the lines, and even though Evelyn didn't come out and say it, I think the rope might be tied to the cause of death. Or maybe there were some signs of an injury."

"Someone strangled Barnaby?" Jo blinked rapidly, her mind whirling. No wonder the investigators tore Gary's house apart. The man's body was found on Gary's property. A watch belonging to Gary was found near the body. If there was a potential murder weapon nearby, the evidence was all there.

Motive and opportunity. There was no doubt Gary and Barnaby knew each other or that they'd had a falling out when Gary discovered that Barnaby had stolen things from him. "This is awful." Jo had a sudden thought. "What kind of rope was it?"

Marlee shrugged. "Evelyn said it was your average construction rope."

Jo tapped her chin thoughtfully. "Does the name Rick Pringle ring a bell?"

"Rick's a local. He owns Pringle Construction. It's more of a handyman-type business. I've had him do a few small jobs around here. He offers twenty-four-hour emergency service." Marlee stared at Jo. "Do you think Rick might be a suspect?"

"I'm not ruling anyone out. According to what Delta and I learned, he's a regular at Half Wall Bar. I'm adding him to my list of potential suspects."

Marlee held up a hand. "Remember, Evelyn didn't come out and say that. It's speculation on my end. How is Gary holding up?"

"As you can imagine, he's stressed out." Jo thought about the pills Nash had found in Gary's jacket pocket. "The name Charlie Golden has also surfaced."

"Everyone knows Charlie. He's been in charge of the chapel and cemetery over at Centerpoint for decades now. He's a little...odd but harmless, I think."

Jo mentioned her conversation with Flo Parlow and Sonny Pabst, the bar patron. "Pabst told us we should chat with Charlie, who was a friend of Barnaby's. When we asked Charlie about Sonny and Rick Pringle, he got upset. From our conversation, I don't think Charlie Golden is too keen on Flo and the bar."

Marlee pursed her lips as she shook her head. "Flo's had her share of problems."

"What sort of problems?"

"She closed down for a while. Flo went through a bad divorce, with both her ex and her airing all their dirty laundry in front of the bar's customers." When pressed, Marlee couldn't remember any other details. "I'm sure you can do an internet search on the place. It was a big deal around town a year or two ago."

Raylene returned to the deli's kitchen. "Sherry had to take care of some customers."

"We'll let you get back to work." Jo thanked her friend for the update before backtracking out of the restaurant. They stopped long enough for Jo to pull Sherry aside and repeat her invitation to come to the farm later if the weather worsened.

It was an easy walk to Miles' theater, which was catty-corner to the deli.

"Check it out." Raylene pointed to the flashing marquee sign above the double set of entrance doors. "Divine Dinner Theater."

"It certainly grabs your attention." Jo followed Raylene inside, where the overwhelming aroma of paint filled the lobby. Sentinel between the entrance and the main theater were gold-colored columns. A vintage three-sided ticket booth sat between the doors.

Ting. Jo wandered over to the ticket booth. She bounced onto the tips of her toes and peered through the glass.

Miles was inside, inspecting some loose wires. She gave the glass a light tap. "Hey, Miles."

Jo's brother pivoted, making a quick turn. "Oh. Hey, Jo."

"Raylene and I were in the neighborhood and thought we would stop by to say hello. Your marquee sign looks great."

"Thanks." Miles stepped out of the booth. "It cost me a pretty penny."

"It catches your attention."

"That was the goal. I'm glad all of the repairs are finally winding down." Miles gave them a rundown of the work he'd done since Jo's last visit. "I'm tackling a few loose ends, and then all I have left is to wait for the grand opening."

"Sherry is looking forward to joining you and the others in the VIP booth."

"I would've invited you to join us, but I don't think you'll all fit."

Jo waved dismissively. "We're thrilled to have front row seats."

"Sherry dropped by here the other day with my favorite sandwich from the deli – pastrami on rye, so I figured I would return the favor, do something nice and invite her to join me."

"And she's a pretty woman, close to your age," Jo pointed out.

Miles grinned. "Really? I hadn't noticed."

"Miles." Jo shook her head.

His smile widened. "Sherry and I are kindred spirits. We're both outsiders if you know what I mean. I hope you don't mind."

Jo pondered his statement. She wanted both Sherry and Miles to be happy. If there was a romance on the horizon, who was she to stick her nose into it? "Do I mind? No. Am I surprised? Maybe a little."

"I met her neighbor, Todd, the other day. He's a nice guy. Kinda quiet, though."

"He is a little mysterious." Jo still had no idea what Todd did for a living, although she did know that he worked from home. "We can't stay long. Like I said, Raylene and I were in the neighborhood and thought we would pop in. There are some bad storms brewing."

"I heard," Miles said. "The trailer park's manager mentioned it this morning when I stopped by the office to grab my mail."

"What will you do?"

"I haven't given it much thought." Miles glanced over Jo's shoulder, and his smile vanished.

A man clad in a black suit, carrying a briefcase, strode across the lobby. "Miles."

"Geffen, I thought you left town."

"Not yet. I've been talking to our...associate, and there's one more issue we need to address before I head out."

"I see." Miles' jaw tightened. "I'm sorry, Jo."

"We were just leaving." Jo took a step back. "I'll give you a call later."

"Jo," the mystery man spoke. "Joanna Pepperdine. You're Miles' sister."

"I am."

"Allow me to introduce myself. I'm Orlando Geffen, Miles' new business partner."

"Business partner," Jo echoed. "I didn't know Miles was looking for a business partner."

"Yes. Uh. I figured it wouldn't hurt to have someone else on board to help run the business," Miles stammered.

"I'm in charge of the finances." Geffen smirked.

"Really?" Jo had recently paid Miles the staggering sum of two million dollars after discovering he was her half-brother, both sharing the same father. If he needed money, it was news to her.

"I hate to cut you off," Miles said hastily, "but I'm sure Orlando needs to finish up so he can head to the airport."

"Yes. Of course." Jo cast the man a quizzical glance before saying her good-byes.

Raylene followed her out. "Did you see how your brother reacted when that guy showed up?"

"Like he wasn't happy he was there. Miles shouldn't need a financial partner. He had plenty of cash on hand to pay for the theater." During the ride home, Jo mulled over Orlando Geffen's surprise visit.

Since Miles' arrival, several odd occurrences had hit Jo's radar. The first was his frequent and unexpected trips out of town. Another happened a few months ago when he'd been injured during one of those trips.

Jo had caught him off guard, asking what had happened. Miles rambled on about how he'd gotten into an accident while driving a rental car.

When pressed, he changed the subject, refusing to discuss it. There had been other minor instances when they had been together, and his phone rang. He would let the call go to voice mail. Seconds later, it would ring again and then again until he'd finally switch the phone off.

She sometimes wondered if her half-brother was living a double life, and she was only seeing one side of it.

Back at the farm, Jo dropped her purse and phone in the office and wandered to the kitchen, where she found Delta buzzing back and forth. "You're back."

"I wanted to be home well ahead of the storms. How's Gary doing?"

"He's all right. I'll be glad when the cops close the investigation and leave Gary alone."

"Me too." Jo had a fleeting thought to remain silent about what Marlee had told her but quickly changed her mind. If she were in her friend's shoes, she would want to know. "Marlee managed to get a small inside scoop on the investigation."

Delta abruptly stopped. "Which is?"

"The investigators found a piece of rope next to Barnaby's body."

"Rope?"

"Construction rope matching some they found in Gary's barn. Reading between the lines, Marlee got the impression that the investigators are leaning toward Barnaby not dying of natural causes."

Delta's frown deepened. "Meaning they think Gary is responsible for Barnaby's death." Her voice rose an octave. "They're going to put my Gary in prison."

"I'm sorry, Delta. I know this doesn't look good right now." Jo told her she was going to do a little online research. "Barnaby had his share of enemies. Something tells me our next move is to figure out who he hung out with, and it all goes back to his favorite hangout – Half Wall Bar. Rick Pringle was also mentioned."

"Pringle owns a construction/handyman type business."

"He's definitely on the radar. Let me help you finish up here, and then we'll start doing some digging around."

The women made quick work of finishing the dinner prep and then made a beeline for Jo's office.

"Let's start with Barnaby Iteen." As soon as the computer was up and running, Jo logged on and typed, "Barnaby Iteen, Divine, Kansas."

A brief article popped up, mentioning him being arrested for breaking and entering. Jo slipped her reading glasses on and read it aloud. "Smith County Sheriff's Department arrested Barnaby Iteen after he was discovered sleeping in the back room of the Four Corners Mini-Mart."

The article went on to say he'd broken in through the back door, helped himself to some ready-to-eat sandwiches, a six-pack of beer and a roll of scratch-off lottery tickets.

"When was that?" Delta asked.

Jo checked the article's date. "Just over a year ago." She clicked out of the screen and scrolled to the bottom of the page. "If he was in trouble with the law like everyone is saying, he managed to somehow keep a fairly low profile."

Delta scooched in. "Let's take a closer look at Half Wall Bar. Sonny Pabst mentioned past problems."

"You read my mind." Jo grew quiet as she typed in the name and location of the bar. The results were like hitting the lottery, the screen quickly filling with articles. The first was about a brawl in the parking lot. Two bar patrons began fighting. One broke free, climbed into his car and attempted to run over the person he was arguing with.

There was another article about the bar's woes, all mixed up in a messy divorce between Flo and her now ex-husband. One of the writers even commented the place was cursed when it suffered extensive damage during a kitchen fire.

"Hmm." Delta leaned over Jo's shoulder as she read the article. "I wonder if Barnaby set fire to Florence's place."

"That would be like burning down your house," Jo joked. "I mean, if he was a regular at the bar, why would he set it on fire?"

They perused a few more articles, all similar reports about marital woes, the fire, some fights, basically rehashing what they'd already gleaned from the previous articles.

"Let's try Charlie Golden," Delta suggested. "The fact that he seemed angry and Pabst, a bar regular, was pointing fingers means there might be something worth digging into."

"True." Jo typed Charlie's name in the search box and hit enter. Nothing popped up. She tried again, this time typing in Centerpoint Chapel. She clicked on the website, touting its "claim to fame" as being the centerpoint of the contiguous United States. A grainy picture of the chapel, the physical address and an email address were at the top of the page.

A "donate now" button was also near the top. She scrolled all the way to the bottom, where the name "Charlie Golden, Caretaker" appeared in tiny letters.

"It's a bust." Jo leaned back in her chair. "We haven't learned anything new."

Delta drummed her fingers on the desk. "Try Rick Pringle. Let's see if we can connect any dots between him and Barnaby."

"Right." Jo typed his name in the screen's search box. A website popped up, listing a variety of services he offered. She scanned the list before clicking out of it. Frustrated, she exited the screen.

"Maybe we're going about this all wrong. Why don't we search the county criminal records?"

"That's a brilliant idea." Jo reached for the mouse and navigated through the screens until she found Smith County's public records. She drilled down until finally finding a search-by-name option. She typed in Barnaby's name first. It was no surprise when several arrest records along with miscellaneous filings filled the screen.

One was linked to Gary's police report. There was also one for the area's convenience store. Other names appeared. Some sounded vaguely familiar but didn't hit Jo's radar until she reached the very bottom. Her heart skipped a beat. "I think we found something."

Chapter 16

Jo perused the limited information regarding Rick Pringle. "Pringle was arrested for assault. The plaintiff was none other than Barnaby Iteen." Her head shot up. "How come we haven't heard about this before?"

"I'm sure the investigators know all about it," Delta said.

"True. So, maybe Gary isn't at the top of the list of suspects. Rick Pringle also had a run-in with Barnaby, *and* he owns a construction-type business," Jo murmured. Her cell phone chirped. She snatched it off the table. "It's Marlee. Hey, Marlee."

"Hey, Jo. I got another tidbit of information. The investigators are out at Half Wall Bar."

"They are?" Jo perked up. Her excitement was short-lived. "It may be nothing. From what I'm hearing, the cops are there a lot."

"But not typically in the early afternoon," Marlee pointed out.

"If Barnaby hung out there half as much as I suspect, then it stands to reason they would want to talk to Flo Parlow, the bar's owner."

"Well, I thought it was interesting."

"It is. Thanks for the heads up."

"I better get back to work. Wait." Marlee stopped her. "One of my customers told me the weather service has issued our area's first tornado watch. You might want to keep an eye on the sky."

"Thanks for the heads up." Jo told Marlee to be safe, to close up and send Sherry home if needed.

"Trust me, I will. These types of storms are nothing to mess with. You stay safe too."

Jo promised her that she would. She ended the call and waved her phone in the air. "The cops are out at Half Wall Bar, and we're under a tornado watch." She reached for the mouse and pulled up the local news station's website. An enlarged map of Kansas filled the screen.

Ominous red blobs were moving west to east. Miniature tornadoes dotted the state, and dark purple splotches were in between the twirling tornadoes.

"It's the finger of God," Delta whispered.

Jo's breath caught in her throat when she realized all of those swirling masses were bearing down on the tiny Town of Divine.

*****

"Those storms are coming right toward us." Jo switched the audio on and turned it up.

"...for supercells to spawn from two major storm systems coming in from the north and south with the potential for dangerous and unstable air masses. We're already receiving reports of damage from Obixon to our west." The meteorologist told viewers to remain vigilant and expect more alerts within the hour.

"Great." Jo swallowed hard. "It looks like we're not going to dodge a bullet this time. Let's give everyone a heads up."

"I'll run over to the bakeshop and mercantile," Delta said.

"And I'll head out back to see if I can track down Gary and Leah before swinging by the housing units."

The women parted ways with Jo hurrying to the gardens. Gary, already noting a change in the weather, was battening down the hatches, securing all loose tools and equipment. He told her the next task was to move the hens to the barn.

He assured her once they were done settling the hens, Leah was free to head to the house while he ran home to secure his property before returning to ride out the storms.

Jo told him to be careful, casting a wary glance skyward. She turned toward the house and then changed her mind. There was still time to check on the beehives. Moving quickly, she took the dirt path leading to the far corner of her property.

Circling each of the enclosures, Jo gave them firm nudges. The new hives Nash had built could easily withstand strong gusts of wind. The beehives weren't going anywhere unless a Wizard of Oz caliber storm struck.

Jo began making her way back, keeping tabs on the swirling clouds overhead. She thought about Miles, who was living in a travel trailer on the outskirts of town.

Pulling her phone from her back pocket, she dialed her brother's cell phone.

"Hey, Jo."

"Hey, Miles. The storms are heading our way. You need to take shelter. Where are you?"

"At the trailer park."

"Please come here where it's safe." She could hear an edge of panic in her voice. She'd only recently discovered she had a brother. She wasn't prepared to lose him now.

"If absolutely necessary, the park's public restrooms and laundry room are solid concrete."

"Are you going there?"

"Probably not. I drove by a few minutes ago, and they're already crowded."

"Then, please come here."

"I...are you sure?"

"Positive. Delta will even feed you."

Miles chuckled. "You twisted my arm. I'm on my way."

"Thank you. Now I'll have one less thing to stress out about."

"I can't have my big sis worrying about me," Miles teased. "Seriously, I'll leave in a few."

"See you soon." Jo pressed the end button. The wind had picked up, whipping stray strands of hair across her face and into her eyes. Drops of rain started to fall. "Dear God. Please protect us."

Jo picked up the pace, passing by the smaller garden, when a movement beyond the barns, near the road and a cluster of trees, caught her attention. As she drew closer, she realized it was two men — two very large men. They were standing motionless, staring at her.

Their light brown hair was long and brushed the tops of their broad shoulders. Their hands were folded in front of them. What could only be described as a radiant glow surrounded them. Although the wind had picked up, their loosely fitted garments didn't move.

A sense of peace filled Jo. It was then that she knew they were Divine's guardian angels.

She took a tentative step closer, half expecting them to fade away, but they didn't. The angels were taller than she remembered. Their shoulders were broad. She was close enough now to note their solemn expressions, compelling yet commanding.

In other words, she wouldn't want to end up on their bad side. There was a power emanating from them, an aura of strength. Jo could feel a surge of energy starting at the top of her head and rushing to her toes.

"Jo," a voice called out from the direction of the housing units. She looked away. Delta was hurrying toward her. When she turned back, the ethereal beings were gone. They were gone, but the surge of energy and strength continued to flow through her body.

Although Jo could no longer see them, she sensed they were still nearby.

She waited for Delta to join her. "I'm calling an early supper. Nash closed the shop after checking the forecast. The residents are collecting their things and will be heading to the house shortly. They're bringing Curtis. She's gonna stay in the main house until the weather settles down."

"Good. Our poor kitty would be scared to death all by herself. Miles is on his way."

Delta leaned in, closely studying her friend's face. "Are you all right?"

"Yes. Why?"

"Your face." Delta waved a hand in front of Jo's face. "It's got a funny glow. I mean, not funny but kinda bright, like you rubbed a glow stick across it." She grasped Jo's hand. "Your hand is as cold as ice."

"I saw them."

"Saw who?"

"Divine's guardian angels. They were right there by that cluster of trees, watching me. I was able to get close to them...close enough to get a good look. When you called my name, they disappeared."

"What did they look like?"

"I..." Jo struggled to describe them. "They were big and bright, giving off a radiant light. I could almost feel their strength." Jo rubbed her arms. "It gave me a surge of energy. In fact, I still sense they're nearby."

"Maybe they're here to protect us from the storms."

"Speaking of storms. Let's head to the house." Jo cast a wistful glance in the direction of the trees, still feeling the presence of the powerful beings.

The residents had already gathered in the living room, along with Duke and Curtis. Nash was there. Gary hadn't returned, and Miles hadn't shown up yet.

The television was blaring loudly. The meteorologist Jo had watched earlier was still on. The storms were tracking closer, and the ticker on the bottom showed them being in line for a direct hit within the next couple of hours.

Jo caught the faint revving of a car's engine. She darted to the door and watched as Gary, with Miles right behind him, strode across the driveway and made their way to the house. "Good. You're both here."

Everyone began talking at once, and Delta let out a low whistle to get their attention. "We're gonna eat dinner early since we might not have power later, not to mention we may be stuck in the cellar." She herded the group into the dining room, where the table was already set.

"Since I didn't have time to finish preparing a proper meal, it's chef's potluck."

There were leftovers from the past couple of nights, including the Italian chicken rollups, some slices of meatloaf and a few of Laverne's seven-layer burritos.

A stack of crispy grilled ham and cheese sandwiches made their rounds, along with bags of chips.

After filling their plates, the room's occupants bowed their heads.

"Heavenly Father," Jo prayed, "please protect us. We pray for our families and loved ones, for those who are in or will be in these storms' paths. We pray for Gary and Delta as they make their way through the stressful days ahead as we prepare for their wedding. Thank you for all of your blessings, and most importantly, for our Savior, Jesus Christ. Amen."

"Amen," the group echoed.

Miles rubbed his hands together. "Delta, this food looks delicious."

"Thank you. I can't take credit for the layered burritos. Laverne made those."

"I'm sure I'll enjoy every bite." Miles passed the plate of leftover rollups to Laverne on his right. "What's this about a death?"

"Barnaby Iteen," Jo said. "You mean you haven't heard about it?"

"Not about his death, but now that you mention it, I have heard the name in passing."

Delta, Gary, Nash and Jo took turns bringing Miles up to speed. Jo shared her suspicions, her plan to delve a little deeper into Barnaby's past to find out more about his habits and how she hoped to start at the Half Wall Bar.

"I know that place," Miles said. "My buddy, Chet, and I go down there about once a week to shoot some pool and blow off steam. Not to mention Flo's kitchen cook makes a mean burger."

Jo's heart skipped a beat. "You know Flo?"

"Yeah. I mean, I don't know Flo well but well enough. She's not what I would call a chummy sort of person, but then I guess you would have to be a little rough around the edges to be a woman running a place like that."

Delta and Jo exchanged a quick glance. They could use someone to do a little digging around…someone who could maybe uncover information in a more conversational way without raising suspicions.

"You wouldn't happen to be going back there anytime soon, would you?" Delta hinted.

Miles reached for his glass of lemonade. "Like I said, I stop by there about once a week, usually on Saturday night. Of course, once I open for business, I'll be too busy." He took a sip, eyeing Delta over the rim. "You've got that look. The wheels are turning," he teased.

"I was thinking that if Jo and I go back to the bar, it will look suspicious. Flo isn't going to talk to us. You, on the other hand, being a semi-regular and all, might be able to do a little intel."

Jo warmed to the idea. "Delta is right. Flo won't be suspicious of you. One of the regulars, Sonny, seemed to know a lot about Barnaby too."

"Sonny Pabst. The bar is his second home. He owns some kind of small business around here. He's there every time I go in." Miles sawed off a chunk of an Italian chicken rollup. Cheese and sauce oozed out. He took a big bite and let out a moan of pure delight. "Delta Childress, you have got to be the best cook."

"You're such a charmer." Delta attempted indifference, but Jo could tell she was flattered by Miles' praise.

"I only charm where charm is due." He took another bite.

"Why, if you did this itty-bitty favor for us, I would make you the juiciest Swiss steak with mouth-watering scalloped potatoes that will ever pass by your lips," Delta promised.

"You're killing me here, Delta." Miles groaned. "You give me some pointers on what you want me to ask, and I'll be delighted to barter a meal in exchange."

"It's a deal." Jo had another thought. "You've been around for a while now. Have you ever heard of Rick Pringle?"

"Yeah. Sure. Rick's a handyman. I've hired him a few times to help me at the theater."

"Delta and I discovered Mr. Pringle was arrested for assaulting Barnaby Iteen, the man who died."

Miles' fork was midair as he paused. "No kidding. Do you think he might have had something to do with this Iteen man's death?"

Jo lifted a finger. "Follow me here. Barnaby does odd jobs. He's not an upstanding citizen or worker, for that matter. Pringle and Barnaby argue. Something happens between them. Pringle is charged with assaulting Barnaby."

"And there was some sort of construction rope found near his body," Delta added.

Gary cleared his throat. "Same kinda rope was found in my barn. It's a common rope. You can buy it over at Wayne Malton's hardware store." His expression grew glum. "I knew I never shoulda let Barnaby sleep in my barn."

Jo perked up. "Sleep in your barn?"

"Only for a coupla weeks – until I found out he was stealing from me. As soon as I kicked him off my property, I padlocked the barn door."

"Do you mind if we run by there to have a look around?" Jo asked.

"Of course not. I doubt you'll find anything, though. The cops have already searched it along with every square inch of my property."

The room's occupants grew quiet as a rumble of thunder shook the house.

"It's getting closer." Michelle slid out of her chair and cautiously approached the window. "The wind is picking up."

Duke, who had been lying in the doorway, scrambled to his feet and joined her. He pressed his snout against the glass and let out a low whine.

"We should finish up and get ready to head down to safety," Nash suggested.

There was an uneasy silence as the room's occupants hurried to finish their meal. The rumbles of thunder increased and grew more intense. Flashes of lightning filled the sky, and the dining room window rattled.

Duke's ears lowered, and he slunk under the table. Curtis let out a yowl and pawed at Leah's leg. She picked the cat up and held her close. "Curtis doesn't like storms."

"She's not alone." Kelli clasped her hands. "Maybe we should check to see how close they're getting."

While Delta and the residents began cleaning up, Jo, Nash, Gary and Miles headed to the living room television. Jo watched in horror as the mini-tornadoes multiplied right before their eyes, continuing on a direct path toward Divine.

If anything, the storm's cone had ballooned. The entire middle and upper section of the state was covered in red.

Sirens blared loudly. "There's been a tornado sighting in Smithville. If you're in Smith County, you need to take cover now."

Chapter 17

Things moved fast as the residents scrambled to safety. Nash and Gary urged everyone to take cover in the cellar.

Jo fell to her knees and crawled beneath the dining room table, attempting to coax her terrified pup out.

Leah, who was still holding onto a terrified Curtis, led the residents down the cellar steps.

While the women made their way to safety, Jo could hear the forecaster repeating his ominous warning. "...take shelter immediately."

Gary and Miles scooped up the emergency supplies and followed the women to the cellar.

Eerie sirens loudly wailed as Jo attempted to grab hold of her terrified pup, who continued to cower under the dining room table.

"Jo! Where are you?" Nash's frantic voice echoed from the kitchen.

"I'm under the dining room table trying to grab Duke."

Nash raced back into the room and joined Jo. Working together, the couple half-carried, half-dragged Duke from his hiding spot.

"Let's go." Nash kept a firm grip on Duke as he propelled Jo into the kitchen.

She slowed as she passed by the window overlooking the side yard. The skies, which had turned an ominous shade of black as debris swirled in the air, mesmerized her.

Tink...tink. Hail began pelting the windows.

A limb on Jo's oak tree bent sideways. It snapped off and fell to the ground.

"Jo, we have to go!" Nash yelled.

"I..." She stood transfixed, staring out the window. The wind suddenly stopped. It was the calm before the fury.

As suddenly as the wind had stopped, it picked up again, except this time, it began swirling, sucking up dirt and tender crops from the adjacent field.

The faint sound of what reminded her of a freight train or roaring waterfall grew louder.

"It's coming." Nash grasped Jo's upper arm with his free hand, dragging her and Duke to the cellar door. They flew down the steps. Nash released his grip on Duke, pausing only long enough to secure the door behind them.

They reached the bottom step and found the residents, Gary and Delta, along with Miles huddled together on a pile of empty burlap bags.

The second set of cellar doors, the ones leading outdoors, were creating an ear-splitting racket. *Crack, crack, crack.*

Jo watched in horror as the doors strained against the force of the wind. Each time they lifted, light could be seen coming through.

Nash wrapped his arms around Jo as she squeezed her eyes shut, praying the doors would hold.

The cracking abruptly stopped, and the doors began making a new sound. *Whomp. Whomp. Whomp.* With each whomp, Jo cringed. It seemed to go on forever before growing fainter and then finally stopping.

"It stopped," Kelli whispered.

Nash motioned for the others to stay put as he rose to his feet and made his way up the cellar steps.

Jo watched as he slid the bolt that secured the double doors and cautiously eased them up. She swallowed hard, bracing herself for a report on the destruction. "Is the house still standing?"

"It is. The storm is moving away. I think we're safe, at least for now."

In a daze, Jo staggered out of the cellar. She followed the others as they made their way onto the lawn.

Downed limbs dotted the yard and driveway. One of the barn doors dangled from its hinges. The decorative flowering planters Jo had placed in front of the bakeshop and faithfully nurtured were on their sides near the end of the drive.

"It doesn't look as bad as I thought it would." Jo walked to the corner of the barn, where she had an unobstructed view of the whole house.

The hanging baskets she'd taken down and placed in the corner of the porch had tipped over, and dirt spilled out. Her stone birdbath, which had been full of water, was bone dry, but it was still standing.

She cast an eye toward the sky, watching as the thick, black clouds continued moving away.

"I don't think we're out of the woods yet." Nash nodded toward the back of the house and another cluster of ominous clouds.

"It looks like it's gonna be a long night," Miles said. "I wonder if my travel trailer is still standing."

Jo could feel tears burn her eyes at the thought of her brother being trapped inside his small trailer, facing the fierce storm all alone. "The trailer can be replaced. You can't."

"I want to check on my chickens." Leah, along with Gary and Delta, headed to the barn while the other residents left to check on their apartments.

Duke led Jo and Nash around the house. With each step she took, Jo thanked God for sparing the farm, for sparing their home.

After going back inside to quickly check the weather report, the couple confirmed their suspicion that they weren't out of the woods yet. Another cluster of cells was moving in their direction.

Remembering how quickly the last storm had hit, Jo and Nash both agreed it was best if they all returned to the cellar.

By the time she and Nash were able to summon everyone, the winds had picked up again. It was déjà vu as the skies grew dark, and hail pelted the windows.

The second round of storms hit with the same ferocity but passed faster than the first.

After it ended, the group emerged to find more limbs down. Several shingles were missing from the shed's roof.

Jo caught a glimpse of blue skies off in the distance and excitedly motioned to the others. "I think the worst of it's over." With a quick check of the weather, she returned outside to give everyone the good news.

Miles stayed long enough to lend a hand cleaning up, and then Jo accompanied him to his car.

"I'm still planning on heading over to the bar to see what I can find out, although I'm not sure how successful my little intel-gathering mission will be," Miles warned.

"Duly noted. All we ask is that you try."

"I was thinking about maybe asking Sherry if she wanted to tag along. She once told me she plays a mean game of pool and even won a little cash in some competitions back in the day."

Jo frowned. "I don't know how I feel about Sherry becoming involved."

"She'll be perfectly safe. You have my word. Besides, two sets of eyes and ears are better than one."

Miles had a valid point. Sherry was sharp, and she might pick up on something he missed. "Since you put it like that, I guess I don't see the harm in her joining you. I can't go into details due to privacy issues, but I don't think it's a good idea for her to be drinking."

Miles placed a hand over his heart. "I promise, we won't be drinking. If I invite her to come along, we'll both stick to sodas."

"All right." Jo relented. If she couldn't trust her brother, who could she trust? As she watched him drive off, an uneasiness settled over her.

Perhaps it was because she had worked so hard – Sherry had worked so hard to escape her troubled past. Hanging out in a bar was something Jo wouldn't recommend to any of her residents.

Delta and Gary made their way over, explaining that they wanted to head to his place to check for damages.

One by one, the residents drifted off, leaving Jo and Nash alone.

"That was a wicked storm." Jo gathered a handful of branches and tossed them in the yard waste bin.

Nash grabbed the container's handle and steered it toward another cluster of downed limbs. "As long as I live in this area, I don't think I'll ever get used to tornadoes."

"I don't think I will either, not after what we just went through. I hope Divine survived the storm." Jo thought about Sherry and excused herself to go give her former resident a call.

Sherry reassured her she was fine, and from a preliminary observation, it appeared Divine had been spared, as well.

Jo reminded her to stay vigilant before joining Nash, who was still cleaning up. "I think I'll run back to check on the gardens."

"Mind if I join you?" Nash reached for Jo's hand.

"Of course not."

The couple rounded the corner and stepped onto the dirt path that led to the back, making their way past Leah, who was standing next to the chicken coop.

As they drew closer, Jo realized Leah wasn't tending to the chickens. Instead, she was staring at a clump of trees, the same ones where Jo had spotted Divine's angelic guardians.

"Hang on." Jo switched directions, and she and Nash joined Leah. "Is everything all right?"

"I...Yes." Leah held out her hand. "Look what I found."

Jo tilted her head, studying the silver cross necklace Leah was holding. "It's a cross necklace. I've never seen that before."

"It's mine. I was wearing it out in the gardens a while back. The chain was kinda long. It got caught on a berry bush and broke." Leah explained that while she and Gary had searched everywhere, they couldn't find it. "How did it get here?"

A chill ran down Jo's spine as she gazed at the trees. "I saw what I believe may have been Divine's guardian angels earlier today. They were standing right there."

"Jo." Leah's mouth dropped open. "Remember when Gary and I saw them out by the fence?"

"I do."

"The day we saw them was the day I lost my necklace. What if the angels found it and returned it to me?" Leah ran a light finger over the cross. "My grandmother gave this to me not long before she died. It was passed down to her from her mother, my great-grandmother. I was heartbroken when it happened, and I prayed..." Leah's voice cracked. "I prayed I would find it."

"Isn't that wonderful? God answered your prayer in the most amazing way."

"The angels are real, Jo."

"Yes, they are."

"I can't wait to tell Kelli." Leah hurried off to share her exciting story.

Jo grew quiet as she and Nash made their way to the gardens, each pondering the miraculous recovery of the cross necklace.

Nash was the first to speak. "It's comforting to think that God cares as much about our little things as He does about our big things."

"Yes, it is."

He changed the subject. "What are your thoughts about Rick Pringle?"

"Barnaby filed charges claiming Pringle had assaulted him. I don't know how I would go about figuring out if there's a connection between Barnaby's death and Pringle." Jo mentioned the construction rope again.

"Pringle owns a small handyman/construction business," Nash said.

"He does. I discovered that when I was checking out his website. He also offers twenty-four-hour emergency services."

"What if we have him come out and quote us on some work?"

Jo snapped her fingers. "Nash, that's brilliant."

"I can be." Nash snuck a kiss. "Which is another reason you need to keep me around."

"Thanks for the reminder." Jo chuckled.

They finished inspecting the gardens. Jo wasn't surprised to find there was minimal damage – much like the house, the residents' units, the workshop, the barn as well, as the garden shed. God had protected them.

Delta and Gary returned a short time later. Similar to Jo's, Gary's place had been spared. He didn't stay long, claiming he wanted to head back to start cleaning up.

The evening light had faded, and Nash and Jo trekked to the porch for their nightly date on the swing.

Jo scooched in and snuggled close to him. Duke, who was still wary from the storms, joined them, hogging half the seat and forcing Jo to cuddle even closer.

"Duke," Jo scolded. "You're turning into a swing hog."

"I taught him to do that," Nash joked. "It's part of my covert plan to force you into my arms."

"You did not." Jo playfully swatted at him.

"Don't be so sure."

They enjoyed the serene evening air, chatting about Gary's investigation and Miles' offer to do a little snooping. The conversation reminded her of earlier when she'd stopped by the theater and ran into Miles' new business partner.

She shared her concern. "Why would Miles need a financial business partner? I know for a fact that he had enough money to purchase the theater and have plenty of cash left over for repairs and startup costs."

"It's none of my business, but now that you brought it up, I've often wondered why he's living in a travel trailer in a campground when he could easily buy a home around here."

"Or add an apartment in the upper level of the theater," Jo said. "Unfortunately, if I ask too many questions, Miles shuts down. I think there's something going on. He's always leaving town suddenly and then returns out of the blue."

"You don't know much about his past," Nash pointed out.

"Perhaps that's by design." Her uneasiness over Sherry accompanying him to the Half Wall Bar returned. "Maybe Sherry shouldn't go with Miles to the bar tomorrow."

Nash squeezed her hand. "I'm sure he's on the up and up about the visit. Besides, he's doing it for Delta and you. Who knows...maybe she won't even go."

"True."

"It's getting late, and it's been a long day." Nash reluctantly stood. "I'll give Pringles Construction a call first thing in the morning to have Rick come out and take a look at the small leak in the workshop sink's drain." Although Nash was handy and could tackle almost any project around the farm, he drew the line at plumbing, insisting that some things needed to be left to the experts.

Jo thanked him and returned inside. She forgot about Miles and Sherry until later when she was getting ready for bed.

She shut the light off and lay there in the dark, thinking about the day and all that had happened, from Aaron Beck's visit to discovering new evidence in Barnaby's death, including the charges against Rick Pringle.

There was also Marlee's call about the police visiting Half Wall Bar. The terrifying tornadoes had passed over the farm, and God had miraculously spared them. And then there was the miracle of Leah's recovered cross necklace.

Last, but not least, was Miles' promised visit to the bar.

Jo reminded herself, once again, that Sherry was an adult. She didn't need Jo's permission to accompany Miles to the bar. And, as Nash pointed out, there was still a chance Sherry couldn't – or wouldn't go with him.

She mulled over Miles' financial partner, Orlando Geffen. Jo was almost certain Miles did not care for the man. Who was he? And why was he Miles' partner?

So many small, nagging bits and pieces of Miles' life didn't add up. Therein lay Jo's biggest concern about a potential relationship between Sherry and him. Did she trust her half-brother? Did she really even know him?

Life experiences had taught Jo that hidden things eventually came to light. She prayed whatever secrets Miles was keeping wouldn't harm him, herself or anyone she loved.

Chapter 18

Sherry beat Jo to the punch, phoning her early the next morning. "Good morning, Sherry."

"Morning, Jo. I...Miles called me last night. He said he was planning on doing a little snooping around over at the Half Wall Bar for you and Delta and invited me to go with him."

"He is."

"And you're all right with that?" Sherry hurried on. "I mean, I know you can't tell me what to do. I also know how you feel about those kinds of places."

Jo chose her words carefully. "I would be lying if I told you I wasn't concerned. I don't particularly want to encourage you to hang out in a place that might tempt you to do things I believe are not in your best interest."

"I'll be with Miles."

"Yes, and I'm sure Miles won't try to convince you to do anything you know you shouldn't." At least Jo hoped so.

"I didn't give him an answer. I told him I would let him know this morning. I wanted to talk to you first."

"I appreciate you valuing my input. The bottom line is that ultimately, the decision is yours."

"I love Delta and Gary, and I want to help them in any way I can," Sherry said. "Besides, I know Florence Parlow. She comes to the deli a couple times a month. I don't think me showing up with Miles would make her suspicious."

Sherry's statement put a new spin on things. If the woman liked Sherry, she might be open to discussing certain things. Possibly even Barnaby Iteen's death. "I think I'll tell Miles yes. He said he planned to report back to you as soon as we left the bar."

The fact Sherry would be stopping by after the snooping gave Jo a degree of comfort. With that in mind, she told Sherry she had her blessing.

Jo wrapped up the call and discovered Delta standing in the doorway. "You gave Sherry the green light to go to the bar with Miles."

"I did. Sherry knows Parlow. She's a people person and has one of those personalities that others are drawn to. We can't pin all of our hopes on her, but there's a chance if there's something, some puzzle piece that would help us, I guess I'm all for it." Jo placed her cell phone on the desk. "Besides, she wants to help you and Gary."

"We need all the help we can get." Delta waited for Jo to join her. She slipped her arm through Jo's, and they strolled to the dining room where everyone sat waiting.

"I'm sorry."

Nash pulled out Jo's chair. "No problem. We're just sitting here, our mouths watering and our stomachs grumbling as we wait to dig into Delta's breakfast feast."

"The breakfast bake looks scrumptious." Jo placed her napkin in her lap and motioned for Gary to say the morning's blessing.

His prayer was heartfelt as he thanked God for sparing Divine from the previous day's storms.

"Amen," the group echoed.

During the meal, Nash and Gary took turns reporting on the damage. After finishing, Leah shared her story about the cross necklace that was hanging around her neck.

"Can we see it?" Michelle asked.

Leah carefully removed the necklace and handed it to her. Michelle rubbed the top with her thumb and passed it to Raylene. "It's been touched by an angel."

Kelli squinted her eyes. "There's a scratch – a cross on the cross."

"Let me see." Leah took the necklace from her and studied it. "You're right. There's almost a perfect cross in the corner."

The necklace circled the table, finally making its way to Laverne, who was seated next to Leah. "I don't see another cross."

"It's there. In the lower-left corner," Leah said.

"Oh...okay, now I see it. That's a sweet fairytale." She handed the necklace to her.

"Fairytale?" Leah pursed her lips. "You don't believe it?"

"Let's just say I think it's a little far-fetched. Angelic beings...a missing necklace suddenly being found not far from where Jo had recently seen them."

"You would believe it if you saw them," Raylene insisted.

"If I do, you'll be among the first to know."

"Laverne." Jo shot her resident a warning glance, and the conversation about angels and the necklace ended.

Nash pulled Jo aside after breakfast. "Rick Pringle is stopping by later today to look for the leak. I figured you might want to join us."

"Yes. I sure do." Jo thanked him before heading to her office. She couldn't shake a nagging trepidation about Orlando Geffen, Miles' business partner.

She turned her computer on and searched several variations of his name's spelling but hit a brick wall with every combination she tried.

As a last resort, she logged into LinkedIn. She struck out again and finally gave up. Orlando Geffen was a mystery man in every sense of the word.

Jo began tackling the task of updating the residents' progress files. Since she'd eaten a hearty breakfast, she decided to skip lunch. After finishing the updates, she began inventorying the mercantile's merchandise and then began studying the bakeshop's recent sales numbers.

Deep in thought, Jo jumped when her cell phone chimed. It was a text from Nash, letting her know Rick Pringle had arrived.

Jo strode out of the office and across the driveway. A utility truck was parked in front of Nash's workshop. The cab's door was open, and as she walked past, she cast a furtive glance inside.

The bench seat was filled with crumpled fast-food wrappers and dirty work gloves. Closer to the passenger seat, grease marks marred the top and sides of a small cooler.

Jo stepped into the workshop's office, where Nash and a balding man sporting a navy blue work uniform stood near the utility sink.

Nash caught Jo's eyes and motioned her over. "Hey, Rick. This is Joanna Pepperdine, the owner."

"Joanna Pepperdine." The man shook Jo's hand, jerking it up and down so hard her head wobbled. "Pleasure to meet you. I've heard lots about you 'round town."

"All good, I hope." Jo let out a sigh of relief when he finally released his grip.

"Yes, ma'am. At least from most people. The rest aren't worth worrying about."

Jo grinned. "My sentiments exactly."

"We already got the little leak fixed," Rick reported. "Nash said you were thinking about installing some extra security equipment in light of the recent string of events."

Jo arched a brow, and Nash winked at her. "Yes. I'm sure you've heard about Barnaby Iteen's body being found. It hits a little close to home."

"Right. Right. I reckon I would be a little concerned too, what with Gary Stein not only working for you but also with his farm being close by."

"Gary did not kill Barnaby Iteen," Jo said bluntly.

Pringle's face grew flushed. "I...I wasn't suggesting he did," he stammered.

Jo forced her voice to remain even. "I'm sorry if I came across as rude. As I'm sure you can imagine, I've had my share of fingers pointed at the women who reside here."

Nash cleared his throat. "We heard Iteen was a handyman-type person. You probably crossed paths in your line of work."

"No. No. Never met the man." Pringle changed the subject, and they began discussing ideas for adding more motion-sensitive lights. After finishing, he excused himself and returned to his truck to write up a quote.

Jo waited until he was gone. "He's lying," she whispered. "I know for a fact that he was charged with assaulting Barnaby."

"It appears your list of suspects is growing."

279

"Unfortunately." Jo blew a breath of air out through thin lips, mentally ticking off the list — Charlie Golden, Florence Parlow, Sonny Pabst and now Rick Pringle. "Iteen was a busy man."

Rick Pringle returned with the quote and briefly went over the itemized charges.

Nash thanked him, and then he, along with Jo, accompanied the man back to his truck. As he pulled away, Jo could see him staring at them in his rearview mirror.

Nash placed a light hand on her shoulder. "What's that saying...motive and opportunity? Rick Pringle oozes both."

"He most certainly does." Jo returned to the house, hoping that Miles and Sherry would be able to glean valuable information and help her narrow down the number of people who might be responsible for Iteen's death.

At ten 'til three, Miles texted, giving her a heads up that he planned to swing by the bar around three. Her earlier uneasiness came flooding back, causing her to second-guess herself. Perhaps she should've encouraged her former resident to take a pass on the snooping.

The bar had more than its share of troubles. The last thing she needed was for Sherry to inadvertently be exposed to a challenging situation.

But it was too late. If Sherry and Miles weren't already there, they were on the way. Now, all Jo could do was pray.

Chapter 19

"After you."

Sherry offered Miles a tentative smile as she stepped inside the bar. It had been years...decades since the last time she'd been inside one. It struck her as being both familiar yet strange.

She wouldn't have given a second thought to hanging out at a bar during her turbulent and troubled past before her incarceration. Now, it was the last place she expected to be. But, she reminded herself, she wanted to help Delta and Gary. They were her family and had done so much for her.

They were one of the reasons she had made it to where she was now, working a steady job, renting an apartment, proving she was capable of living independently and last, but not least, her future was promising. If she could help Miles uncover clues about what had happened to Barnaby Iteen, then she was all in.

Sherry squared her shoulders, following Miles as they strode past several patrons seated at the bar. She could feel the stares as they made their way to the pool tables in the corner.

The woman behind the bar shot them a quick look. "Hey, Miles."

"Afternoon, Flo."

Flo did a double-take. "Sherry Marshall. Marlee cut you loose for the day?"

Sherry could feel herself relax as she recognized the familiar face. "Yes, today is my day off."

Flo propped her elbow on the bar, her gaze flitting from one to the other. "I didn't know you two knew each other."

"Miles' theater is across the street from Marlee's deli," Sherry explained.

"Ah. You're right." Flo lifted a brow. "Welcome to the Half Wall Bar. What can I get you?"

"We'll take a couple cokes if you don't mind. Sherry claims she shoots a mean game of pool, so I challenged her to see if she deserves the bragging rights." Miles winked at Sherry, and she could feel warmth spread from her head to the tips of her toes.

"Two cokes, it is." Flo filled two glasses and carried them over. "Since Sherry always takes such good care of me when I'm at the deli, the drinks are on me."

"Thanks, Flo."

"You're welcome." Flo returned to the bar to wait on a new arrival.

Miles lifted his glass as his eyes traveled around the room. "One of our targets is seated at the bar." He gave a nod of his head before casually setting his coke on a nearby table. "Let's stop by to say hello."

Miles placed a light hand under Sherry's arm and led her across the room. "Hey, Sonny."

"Miles Parker." Sonny sipped his beer, eyeing them over the rim of his mug. "Who's your pretty friend?"

"Sherry Marshall. Sherry, this is Sonny Pabst."

"How do you do." Sonny's cold, clammy hand clasped hers, and she fought the urge to pull away.

"Sherry works at Marlee's deli in downtown Divine."

"You don't say. I didn't know Marlee had such pretty gals working for her," Sonny flirted. "I guess I need to get out more."

"Careful there, Sonny," Miles joked. "She's here with me."

The trio made small talk for a few moments before the couple returned to the other side of the bar.

While Miles set the balls, Sherry perused the sticks.

After finishing, he joined Sherry. "This stick looks lucky." He reached past her, so close she could smell his woodsy-scented cologne. He smelled nice. Her heart rate kicked up a notch as their eyes met. "I'll have to keep a close eye on Sonny. I think he's fallen in love at first sight," Miles teased.

"He needs glasses," Sherry joked.

"I disagree."

Sherry could feel her face turn red. Embarrassed, she made a quick turn and collided with the corner of the pool table.

"Are you okay?" Miles rushed forward. "I'm sorry. I didn't mean to make you uncomfortable," he apologized.

"I...I'm not used to getting compliments," Sherry stuttered.

Despite Miles' apology, the offhanded compliment hung in the air, and Sherry forced herself to focus on the pool game. Her first few shots were duds, but she quickly got into her groove and began pocketing each of her balls.

She barely beat Miles in the first game. The second game was a blowout. In fact, Miles never even got a chance to play.

Sonny stumbled over, beer in hand, as she knocked off the last few balls. He let out a low whistle. "You're good."

"Thank you. It's been a while."

"You live 'round here?" Sonny slurred.

"I do."

Miles held up his hand. "It's probably not wise for a woman to be telling an almost complete stranger where she lives."

"I...I'm not a stranger." Sonny spun around, almost losing his balance, his beer sloshing over the rim and spilling onto the floor. "Hey, Flo!"

"Yeah, Sonny!" she hollered back.

"You can vouch for me. Tell this pretty lady I'm a good guy."

"Sonny's a good guy."

"See?" He spun back around, lurching sideways and his hand fumbling as he grappled to steady himself.

"I live in the area," Sherry said. "I suppose it's best to leave it at that since the police found that poor man's body a couple days ago. Rumor is he didn't die of natural causes."

Sonny blinked rapidly, struggling to focus. "I don't wanna speak ill of the dead, but Barnaby made his share of enemies. Gary Stein took him out, right, Flo?" He staggered back, clutching what was left of his beer. "Barnaby wasn't an upstanding citizen like the rest of us. Him and the crazy dude out at the cemetery. Now, that one is cuckoo." He attempted to twirl his finger next to his forehead. Instead, he lost his balance and almost poked himself in the eye.

"What man at the cemetery?" Sherry asked.

"Crazy Charlie Golden. The cops were out there questioning him the other day. Next thing you know." Sonny attempted to snap his fingers. "They show up here."

"I heard Barnaby was a regular," Miles said. "Of course, the police would stop by."

Flo brought two more glasses of coke to Miles and Sherry. "Now, Sonny. We'll leave the cops to handle their business. Don't be bothering Miles and Sherry with your crazy theories."

"They're not crazy," Sonny insisted. "Golden...that's who's crazy."

Miles and Sherry exchanged a quick glance. Sonny had been a virtual wealth of information – except none of it added up, but if what Sonny had said was true, perhaps Jo and Delta needed to take a closer look at Charlie Golden.

Flo grabbed their empty glasses and led Sonny back to the bar.

The couple played another game of pool. Miles managed to beat Sherry, but not by much. She insisted it was because Pabst was throwing her game off. He kept staring at her in a way that made her skin crawl.

Miles must've noticed it too. "We're drawing some unwanted attention. Flo's cook makes the best burgers. Let's head to the back for a bite to eat."

He escorted her to a booth in the corner of the restaurant section, far from Pabst's prying eyes.

Sherry grabbed a menu from the holder and studied the selection. "Everything sounds good. I can't remember the last time I ate out. Thank you for inviting me."

"You're welcome. We'll have to do it again." At Miles' suggestion, she ordered Half Wall Bar's Hall of Fame burger that came with a side of fries.

Sherry excused herself for a quick trip to the ladies' room to wash up. When she emerged, she found Miles chatting with a man. He left before Sherry got back to the table. "Another regular?"

"Sort of. That was Dex, Flo's son." The man stepped behind the kitchen area and reached into the fridge. Sherry caught his eye. The look he gave her caused a shiver to run down her spine. "What is it about these bar people?"

"It appears you've captured Dexter's attention too."

The food arrived hot and fast. Sherry devoured the thick, juicy burger, insisting it was one of the tastiest she'd ever had. Unable to finish her fries, she offered them to Miles.

Flo stopped by to check on them midway through the meal, and Sherry complimented her on the delicious food. By the time they finished, the bar was filling up, and the pool table they'd been using was occupied.

Miles challenged Sherry to a final game. As the hour wore on, the room grew even more crowded and filled with cigarette smoke.

Sherry attempted to steer clear of it, but her eyes were beginning to burn.

Miles noticed her discomfort and made his way over. "I think it's time to go."

"Yes." Sherry nodded, blinking rapidly. "It's a little smoky for me."

Miles stopped by the bar to thank Flo for the drinks and joined Sherry, who stood waiting by the door. He was the first to speak when they reached the car. "Sonny spent a lot of time watching you."

"Yeah. I noticed it too, and it was creeping me out." Sherry rubbed the sides of her arms. "Did you catch what he said? He seems to think some guy by the name of Charlie Golden might have more information about Barnaby Iteen."

"I heard it too." Miles checked the rearview mirror before backing out of the parking spot. "Hopefully, what we found out will help. In the meantime, we need to report back to Jo and Delta and let them know I kept you safe from Sonny's evil clutches."

"Very funny." Sherry playfully punched him in the arm, casting him a sly side glance. "You were holding out on me. You're a pretty good pool player."

"Maybe a little." Miles grinned. "Coming from you, I'll take that as a compliment."

The trip flew by as Miles and Sherry talked about living in Divine and Miles' theater. She was impressed by his detailed plan for its success.

Caught up in their conversation, she was surprised they had reached the farm so quickly. Sherry ducked down to grab her purse and felt the car lurch as Miles tapped the brakes. "This can't be good."

Sherry's head shot up as she stared out the windshield. "What in the world?"

Chapter 20

A small crowd formed a semi-circle around the front of Nash's workshop. An ambulance was parked off to the side.

Miles had barely come to a stop when Sherry sprang from the vehicle and ran over to Raylene, who was standing nearby. "What's going on?"

"Michelle's been hurt. She was hit in the head by a piece of wood, and it knocked her out."

Sherry craned her neck, catching a glimpse of two EMTs kneeling next to Michelle while Nash, Gary, Delta and Jo hovered nearby.

There were hushed murmurs as the emergency workers continued speaking with Michelle. Finally, they helped her to a sitting position, and one of them removed the blood pressure cuff.

The other flashed a light into her eyes. The men positioned themselves on either side of her, slowly helping her to her feet. The crowd parted as the EMTs escorted Michelle out of the building.

Jo ran ahead and stood waiting for them on the porch steps while Gary, Nash and Delta followed close behind. They reached the house and made their way inside.

Laverne strolled over, shaking her head. "I knew it. This place is an accident waiting to happen. I'm surprised OSHA hasn't come by here to inspect the working conditions."

"What do you mean, it is an accident waiting to happen?" Raylene demanded. "Nash is extremely safety-conscious."

Laverne gave them a rundown of what she thought needed to be done to make the work environment safer. Sherry let her ramble on until she got to the part where she thought they needed to add floor signage and a lighted walkway.

"I'm sure Nash would be open to your input. However, from what I understand about what just happened, he was following all of the safety protocols. Michelle was wearing appropriate safety equipment and following safety guidelines."

Laverne lifted a brow.

Raylene shot her an irritated look. "It was an accident."

"You're entitled to your opinion. I'm entitled to mine." Laverne sniffled loudly and stalked off.

Sherry watched her leave. "Is she always like that?"

"Thankfully, no. Only when Laverne gets a bee in her bonnet about something." Raylene changed the subject. "What brings you to the farm?"

"Miles and I were helping Delta and Gary with a small project. We're here to report back."

"That's right. Delta bribed Miles by promising him a Swiss steak dinner," Raylene teased.

"I would've done it anyway, but don't tell Delta." He smacked his lips. "I even dreamt about the dinner last night."

The trio began making their way to the house, joining the EMTs, Nash and Jo, who were on their way out.

The emergency workers had a brief word with Jo before returning to the ambulance and driving off.

"Is Michelle going to be okay?" Sherry asked.

"She is. She's suffered a concussion." Jo explained that Michelle would be staying with her and Delta until she had recuperated.

Nash cast an anxious glance toward the house. "I feel terrible about what happened."

"It was an accident." Jo patted his arm.

"I'm sure Michelle doesn't blame you," Gary chimed in.

There was some discussion about reviewing the safety policies, and then Nash headed back to the workshop.

Jo turned her attention to Sherry and Miles. "I see you survived your information gathering mission."

"We did. It was kinda fun." Sherry elbowed Miles. "I even let Miles win a game of pool."

"You did not." Miles laughed. "I won fair and square."

"True enough." Sherry sobered. "We did have a nice time, but it wasn't all fun and games."

The couple took turns telling Jo, Gary and Raylene what had happened.

"So, Sonny was deep in his drink and told you he thought Charlie Golden was crazy," Jo summarized.

"That's our take on it," Miles said. "Reading between the lines, he was suggesting the reason the cops showed up at Half Wall Bar was because of something Charlie had told them."

"Which may or may not be true," Jo pointed out. "Barnaby was a regular at the bar."

"I got the impression that there's no love lost between Sonny and Charlie." Sherry shifted her feet.

"Sonny was flirting with Sherry," Miles said. "He even asked her where she lived."

Jo's eyes grew wide. "You didn't tell him, did you?"

"No. Miles pretty much told him it was none of his business."

Delta hustled out of the house. "What did I miss?"

"Sonny Pabst flirted with Sherry. He seems to think Charlie Golden had something to do with Barnaby's death. Maybe we should pay him another visit," Jo suggested.

"Golden was acting kinda funny when we were there. He might know more about Barnaby's past than he's letting on. I reckon it wouldn't hurt to have another chat with him."

Jo turned her attention to Miles and Sherry again. "Was Flo working?"

"Yep."

"How did she act?"

"Like she was trying to corral Sonny." Miles held up an imaginary beverage and took a drink. "Sonny was hitting it pretty hard. She was trying to reel him in. The bar was busy, so we were only able to briefly talk to her."

"Thank you for trying. We appreciate what you were able to find out," Jo said.

"And on that note, I think it's time to head home."

Jo gave Sherry a warm hug. "I'm proud of you."

"I have to admit, I was a little freaked out when I first walked in there." Sherry sucked in a breath. "All in all, we had a good time. Miles even bought me a burger and fries."

Delta muscled her way in for a hug. "Sherry Marshall, you have made us proud. You breezed through another hurdle without giving it a second thought."

"You're right." Sherry beamed. "I did."

"Hey, what am I? Chopped liver?" Miles joked.

"Thank you." Delta impulsively hugged him. "And I owe you that juicy Swiss steak. Let me know when you can come by for dinner again."

"I'll be sure to do that." Miles and Sherry returned to his car and drove off.

Delta shaded her eyes as they pulled onto the road. "Miles likes Sherry," she sing-songed.

"He does."

"What are your thoughts on it?"

Jo pondered the question. On the one hand, she was happy for Sherry. On the other hand, she wasn't one hundred percent certain about her brother based on his semi-suspicious behavior and secretiveness.

It could be that she was being paranoid. There were a lot of things in Jo's past she didn't share with him. Miles was under no obligation to share his. Still...there was the "business partner" who sent up the red flags.

"We'll have to wait and see," Jo finally said.

Marlee arrived a short time later. With everything that was going on, Jo had completely forgotten she planned to stop by to go over some final details regarding the food for the wedding. While Gary and Delta led Marlee across the yard to the barn, where the wedding reception and celebration would take place, Jo ran upstairs to check on Michelle.

Her bedroom door was ajar. Jo gave it a light rap, and when she heard a muffled reply, she slipped inside. Michelle was semi-reclined, the television remote in hand, although the television was turned off. "Hey, Jo."

"Hey, Michelle." Jo perched on the edge of the bed. "How are you feeling?"

"Like someone clobbered me in the head with a two by four."

"I bet." Jo studied the side of Michelle's forehead and the lump that was starting to turn a dark shade of purple. "Delta will be along shortly to hover over you," she teased.

"She's already done that, insisting on making me some homemade chicken noodle soup and hot tea." Michelle clutched the covers to her chest. "I'm sorry, Jo. I didn't mean to get hurt. I hope the ambulance doesn't cost too much. Those guys were here for a while."

"Michelle," Jo's voice grew soft. "I'm glad they were here and that you're going to be all right.

There's absolutely no reason to apologize. I feel bad it happened, and Nash feels terrible."

"Nash had nothing to do with it. He's always careful. The board slipped."

"It was an accident. No one is getting blamed. Not Nash. Not you." Jo patted her leg. "All you need to worry about is making a complete recovery."

"Thanks. I am feeling a little dizzy. The EMTs said it was okay to sleep, so I think I might try to get some rest."

"That would be best. Either Delta or I will be back to check on you." Jo eased off the bed, offering a prayer for Michelle's healing as she tiptoed out of the room.

She headed back out and joined Marlee, clipboard in hand, who stood in the doorway of the barn, along with Gary and Delta.

"How's it going?"

"Hey, Jo. We're finalizing the dinner menu. What are your thoughts about grazing tables?"

"Grazing tables?"

Marlee explained the hot new trend in weddings was grazing tables, a more casual approach to the celebratory meal. "My crew and I would set up small stations all over the barn. She tucked the clipboard under her arm. "We could put an appetizers station over here with veggies and dip, maybe some sweet and sour meatballs and chicken wings."

She strolled to the next corner. "Over here, we could serve finger sandwiches, perhaps platters of mini-barbeque tacos and even some sliders." Marlee suggested a location for desserts, including a designated spot for the wedding cake.

The fourth and final corner would be the location of the beverage station.

Jo pointed at Delta and Gary. "I can give you my opinion, but what do you think?"

"I like it," Gary said. "I'll be happy no matter what's decided, as long as I have my beautiful bride by my side."

Delta beamed as she slipped her arm through his. "That's one of the sweetest things you've ever said."

"Cuz it's true."

"I like the idea, although I wouldn't mind adding some stick-to-your-ribs foods," Delta said.

"You read my mind," Marlee said. "A selection of pasta salads, potato salads, the heavier salads would work well."

"All this talk about food is making me hungry." Gary patted his stomach.

"I brought some sample dishes for you to try." On their way to the kitchen, Marlee swung by her van to grab a to-go carrying case.

Sample sandwiches and the mini-barbeque tacos she'd mentioned, along with small tasting dishes of pasta salad, macaroni salad, potato salad and coleslaw, were inside the case.

She'd also brought a tray of appetizers. "I didn't bring desserts since Delta told me those would come from your bakeshop."

"The residents have some special ideas in mind," Jo confirmed.

They took turns sampling the goodies with Delta and Gary giving Marlee feedback.

After finishing, Gary slowly stood. "I gotta head back to the gardens. Thanks for coming by, Marlee."

"You're welcome." Marlee began gathering the empty containers. "How is the investigation into Barnaby Iteen's death going?"

"It's not. The investigators tore my place apart. I reckon they don't have enough to charge me with, or else they would've arrested me by now."

Marlee finished packing the bag and zipped it shut. "How do you think Iteen's body got onto your property?"

"Someone knew me 'n Barnaby had it out and figured my place was as good as any to hide his body."

"I'm sure the authorities will get to the bottom of it." Marlee patted his arm. "You hang in there."

Gary thanked her again and lumbered off, leaving Delta and Jo to help Marlee carry the containers to the car. "I didn't want to say anything in front of Gary, but the buzz around town is that an arrest will be made soon."

Jo's heart plummeted. "You're kidding."

Delta clutched her chest. "Gary can't go to jail. He's getting married. We're looking forward to that happily ever after part."

"I'm sorry, Delta. I'm not sure who they're targeting, but based on what I've heard, I think it might be Gary."

"It looks like we have no choice but to pay another visit to Charlie Golden," Jo said grimly.

"Let me know if there's anything I can do to help." Marlee shot Delta a sympathetic smile as she climbed into her vehicle. "Since you've already visited Charlie Golden, I'm sure you've figured out that he isn't much of a talker. If your plan is to pump him for information, you might want to invite Carrie Ford to tag along."

"Carrie mentioned his name when she was here the other day."

Marlee pulled her door shut and rolled the window down. "Carrie and Charlie dated some years back, right before she got tangled up with Craig Grasmeyer. I always thought they made the perfect couple. I'm not sure what happened."

"Carrie doesn't seem to have much luck with men. Thanks for the tip. I'll give her a call." After Marlee drove off, Jo turned to Delta. "We better kick this investigation into high gear. I'll grab my purse."

She turned to go, and Delta stopped her. "If you don't mind, I don't want to say anything to Gary about what Marlee said."

"Regarding the arrest."

"His poor old ticker can't take much more of this stress," Delta said. "Besides, we don't know if the authorities are zeroing in on Gary or someone else."

Jo didn't say it, but she was beginning to think Gary being cleared as a suspect was wishful thinking on their part. The fact the type of rope found near Iteen's body was also found in Gary's barn, along with the watch, was probable cause. She wasn't sure what criteria had to be met, but if anyone was close to meeting it, Gary was. "I'll call Carrie."

Back inside, Jo grabbed her cell phone and dialed Carrie's number. When she didn't answer, Jo left her a message and then joined Delta, who was waiting by the SUV. "Carrie's not answering."

"She's probably holed up in her taxidermy shop. She won't answer the phone when she's working on one of her 'creations.'"

"I say we take our chances and swing by her place." Jo took the back roads, skirting the downtown area as she made her way to Serenity Lane, an upscale neighborhood full of meticulously manicured yards and sprawling Tudor-style estates.

The neighborhood was a complete contrast to Carrie's home with its cotton candy pink shutters and bright yellow siding that was reminiscent of the game Candyland.

"That bumblebee yellow siding is burning my retinas," Delta joked. "I'm going to take a wild guess and say that Carrie's choice of colors is her HOAs worst nightmare."

Jo parked near the curb, and she and Delta headed to the small building adjacent to Carrie's pink garage. A faint grinding sound echoed from within.

"Sounds like she's here." Jo gave the door a sharp rap.

The noise continued.

"She can't hear you," Delta said.

Jo tried the handle. The door was unlocked. She eased it open and stepped inside, where they found Carrie standing at the counter, her back to them.

Jo waited until the grinding stopped before reaching behind her and rapping on the door again.

Carrie spun around, sporting face gear that reminded Jo of a combination dive mask and a surgical mask. "Jo. Delta. I didn't know you were stopping by."

"I left a message on your cell phone. Do you have a minute?"

"Sure. C'mon in."

Delta made a gagging sound. "No offense, but I'll wait by the door where I can breathe fresh air."

"It's the formaldehyde. The smell does take some getting used to."

Jo forced herself to ignore the pungent pickle smell. "We heard that you and Charlie Golden are...were friends. He wasn't keen on talking to us the last time we visited him and were wondering if you had time to run by the chapel with us."

"You want to visit Charlie?" Carrie peeled off her mask, revealing deep indents around her eyes.

Delta frowned. "Your face."

Carrie absentmindedly touched her cheeks. "They'll go away in an hour or so. It keeps the flying particles out of my eyes."

"We need Golden to tell us what he knows about Iteen," Delta said bluntly.

"I haven't spoken to Charlie in years. I'm not sure he would be particularly receptive toward me. When were you planning on going?"

"Now."

Carrie stared at Delta. "Right now?"

"Marlee heard a rumor that the investigators are close to making an arrest in Barnaby's death. We think there's a chance they'll be coming after Gary. We're running out of time." Jo clasped her hands. "Will you help us?"

"Of course. Give me a minute to clean up."

Delta and Jo waited by the door while Carrie made quick work of cleaning up. She excused herself to grab her purse and lock the house up.

They returned to the SUV and stood waiting in the driveway...and waited...and waited.

Delta checked her watch. "What happened to that woman?"

"I'll go find out." Jo slipped her keys in her pocket and made her way to the front door. Moments later, she returned to where Delta stood waiting. "Carrie's not answering her door. She went inside the house, right? I mean, we watched her go into the house."

"We did. Call her cell phone," Delta suggested. "Maybe she forgot."

"How could she forget?"

"We're talking about Carrie here."

Jo reached for her phone when she noticed the side door open. Carrie stepped onto the stoop.

Delta pressed her hands to her cheeks. "Heavens to Betsy...err...Carrie."

Chapter 21

Jo wasn't sure how Carrie had managed it, but her cropped curly blond locks were teased, circling her head with a big, black bow tied at the top.

She'd swapped out her grungy t-shirt, paint-spattered khaki capris and steel-toed workboots for a hip-hugging pair of black leather pants, a revealing hot pink blouse and stiletto heels.

She tottered down the driveway and joined them, the overpowering smell of white musk, vanilla and mint oozing from her pores.

"Whoa." Delta made a gagging sound as she waved her hand over her face. "Did you shower in eau de toilette?"

"Oh what?" Carrie's thick layers of bangles and bracelets loudly clanged as she tugged on the bottom of her blouse.

"Cheap perfume."

"I do not wear cheap perfume," Carrie haughtily replied. "I'll have you know Pink Parisian costs almost a hundred dollars an ounce."

"I think you look nice," Jo said kindly.

"Thanks."

Delta muttered something under her breath, and Jo shot her a warning look. "Carrie is doing us a favor," she reminded her.

The trio climbed into Jo's SUV with Carrie taking the back seat. During the drive, Delta created a makeshift mask, using the collar of her shirt.

Admittedly, Carrie's scent was overpowering, and by the time they reached the cemetery, Jo's head was throbbing, and her nose was clogged.

She parked next to a rusted gray car, not far from the entrance to Centerpoint's Chapel. "That must be Charlie's car," Jo said.

"It is. Charlie's been driving that old rust bucket for years now." Carrie pulled a compact from her purse and gave herself the once over. She tossed it back in her bag and removed a travel-size perfume bottle.

"More perfume?" Delta fumbled for the door handle.

"I need a spritz, a refresher," Carrie insisted as she began spraying herself.

Jo sprang from the SUV, leaving the door open as the woman sprayed her hair, her back, her neckline. She finished with a generous spritz to both wrists.

Delta tapped the top of the SUV, motioning to Jo. "You're gonna need an ozone machine to air this thing out."

"It is a little strong." Jo pressed the master window control, rolling down all four windows.

"Almost ready." Carrie plumped up her bosom and then scooched out of the backseat. "How do I look?"

"Like you're ready to stand on a…"

Jo cut Delta off. "…stage for a major production." She led the way along the sidewalk and to the chapel's entrance. The door was locked, and no one was around. "Charlie must be over by the cemetery."

Carrie clasped the front of her blouse as she leaned forward, frowning at her stilettos. "I wasn't planning on doing a lot of walking. I'll just wait here."

"You two stay put. I'll be right back." Delta didn't wait for a reply and stalked off.

Carrie leaned against the side of the SUV. "She doesn't like me very much."

"Delta?"

"Yeah. She's always mean to me."

"Delta likes you. It's just..." Jo knew what Carrie meant, and as much as she loved Delta, she could be brusque and judgmental at times. But she had a heart of gold, and she didn't mean most of what she said, at least not in a mean way.

Delta spoke what was on her mind without giving it a second thought. "She speaks what she thinks without considering how it might hurt someone's feelings. I wouldn't take it personally, Carrie."

"She's unfiltered."

Jo chuckled. "That's a good way of putting it. Delta is unfiltered."

Before Carrie could reply, Delta crested the small incline. Charlie Golden, his mouth set in a grim line, wasn't far behind her.

Out of the corner of her eye, Jo caught a glimpse of Carrie making another "adjustment."

Carrie nervously cleared her throat as they approached. "Hello, Charlie."

"Hey, Carrie. What're you doing here?"

"My friends, Jo and Delta, asked me to come here with them."

"Because you just happened to be in the neighborhood?"

"We're here to ask you a few more questions about Barnaby," Jo explained. "Rumor has it the investigators are getting ready to make an arrest. We think Gary Stein is at the top of their list."

"I'm sorry to hear that."

Carrie squeezed past Jo. "You and Barnaby were friends, perhaps better friends than he was with anyone else. We were hoping you might be able to tell us if he had any enemies, someone who hated him enough to kill him."

"The cops already asked me all of that stuff. I'll tell you the same thing I told them. Not many people liked Barnaby. He spent a lot of time scheming, trying to figure out how to make quick cash and not always by legal or ethical means."

Charlie told them he tried talking to Barnaby to convince him to change his ways. "I thought he might be ready to change until one of the last times I saw him."

"He was reverting back to some bad habits," Jo prompted.

"Maybe. Barnaby said he was working on something big. He said, 'Charlie, I got a sweet deal in the works. Powerful people are gonna pay me money to keep my trap shut.' When I asked him who, he wouldn't tell me, just that he was cooking up something big and seemed to think it was going to put him on Easy Street."

"Instead, it got him killed."

"It's possible." Charlie shrugged. "Not long after he told me that, he disappeared."

"Powerful people were going to pay him money," Jo mused. "So, he was blackmailing someone."

"Considering what I know now, that would be my guess. In fact, I told the cops the same thing."

"Did he have any other friends he hung out with?" Delta asked.

"Nope. Just me and a bunch of regulars down at the Half Wall Bar." Charlie shifted his feet. "I think he hung out with Sonny Pabst and a couple others."

"Do you think Florence Parlow might be involved?"

"I don't know her well. Barnaby liked her, said she took him in a time or two and let him do odd jobs around the business after she split up with her husband."

"Which was right around the time he disappeared."

Charlie paused as he thought about it. "Yeah. Now that you mention it, Barnaby did start doing some odd jobs around that time. He was an opportunist."

"You mentioned Rick Pringle the last time we were here," Jo reminded him. "Did Barnaby ever mention an altercation with him?"

"Yep. The cops asked me about Pringle too. I didn't know him, but Barnaby did some work for him – handyman stuff. And the only reason I know is because he showed up one day with a black eye. Said Rick Pringle punched him."

"Did he say why Pringle hit him?" Delta asked.

"Nope." When pressed, Charlie couldn't remember much else.

"Speaking of injuries, what happened to your face?" Carrie pointed to a bruise near Charlie's jawline.

Charlie gingerly touched it. "Those darn kids keep messing around out here. One of them caught me the other night on my way out after locking up the church. Came around the corner and clobbered me with a board or something. I was able to get a crack at him, and he was limping when he ran off."

"That's terrible. It sounds like the authorities need to step up the patrols around here."

"I was gonna use my taser on him, but he hot-footed it out of here so fast I didn't have time."

Carrie's hand flew to her lips. "Did you call the cops?"

"I did. Unfortunately, I couldn't give them much of a description. The guy was wearing a ski mask, so I couldn't see his face."

"Are you sure it was a teenager? I can't imagine one being savvy enough to hide their identity behind a ski mask." Jo wrinkled her nose.

"Now that you mention it, the kids usually wait until after I'm gone at night to start messing around. Seems to me they're getting braver."

"Well, be careful." Jo thanked him and turned to go.

"Hey." Charlie stopped them and motioned to Carrie. "You're lookin' real good, Carrie. I like your hair."

Carrie beamed as she patted her teased locks. "This old mess?"

"Looks like you've been working out too."

"The taxidermy business keeps me hopping. I've also been spending time at the gym."

"I wouldn't mind seeing your shop sometime."

Jo motioned to Delta, and they quietly slipped away, making their way back to the SUV. Charlie and Carrie didn't appear to notice.

"He's digging her," Delta whispered.

"I think she's digging him right back," Jo said in a low voice.

The tinkle of Carrie's laughter filled the air. She leaned in to say something.

"She had better be careful, or her girls are going to spring free."

"Delta." Jo grinned.

"I'm serious."

Finally, the couple's conversation ended. Carrie gave Charlie a flirty wave and wobbled over. Her cheeks were bright red, and she was taking short little breaths. "Sorry. I didn't mean to keep you waiting."

"No problem." Jo opened the rear passenger door for her. "So?"

"So what?"

"You and Charlie."

"Oh." Carrie dismissively waved as she reached for her seatbelt. "I invited him to stop by with some taxidermy stuff."

"Mmm. Hmm," Delta said. "He was very complimentary."

"Charlie's a sweetheart."

"At the risk of being nosy, it seems like you two would be perfect for each other," Delta said. "What happened?"

"You are being nosy." Carrie sniffed.

Jo chuckled as she shifted into reverse. "You don't have to tell us what happened. I'm glad to see you're speaking again."

"Me too." Carrie changed the subject. "Do you think what Charlie told us might help?"

"I don't know. I'm beginning to think we need to take a closer look at Rick Pringle. I wonder what the 'big deal' was." Delta sucked in a breath. "I can't help but think we're going in circles, chasing our tails."

"No." Jo tightened her grip on the steering wheel. "I don't think so. Other than Rick Pringle, who is going to the top of the list, I think our next step is to focus our attention on the Half Wall Bar."

Chapter 22

Jo's first stop was Carrie's place to drop her off. During the drive home, Delta came up with the idea to search Gary's barn for clues. But first, they needed to get the keys.

It didn't take long to track Gary, who was working in the larger of the two gardens, down. "Well? How did your chat with Charlie go?"

Delta briefly filled him in. "It seems we have two avenues to explore...one is Rick Pringle, and the other is Half Wall Bar."

"You mentioned Barnaby was staying in your barn before you discovered he was stealing from you," Jo reminded him.

"Yep."

"Delta and I would like to take a look around if you don't mind."

"Course not. Delta has a key to the house. The barn keys are hanging on the hook near the back door."

The women turned to go, and Gary stopped them. "I doubt you'll find anything. The investigators already searched it. I did remember one other thing, though." He told them that after he and Barnaby had the falling out, the man was adamant about getting back inside the barn. "When I refused, he was fit to be tied. I don't know why he was making such a fuss. All he left behind was a bunch of junk that I ended up throwing away."

"It's still worth a try."

On their way to the SUV, they ran into Raylene. "How's the investigation shaping up?"

"There are a lot of signs pointing to Half Wall Bar. Unfortunately, we don't know who or why." Jo filled her in on what Charlie had said, how Barnaby hinted at blackmailing someone. "We're on our way over to Gary's place. We figured it wouldn't hurt to check out the barn since he'd let Barnaby stay there."

"Mind if I join you? I'm done working my shift."

Raylene, a former bounty hunter, was the perfect person to help. In fact, Jo was surprised she hadn't thought of her before. "We can always use your expertise and input."

After a quick stop upstairs to check on Michelle, they drove to Gary's place.

Raylene stepped out of the vehicle and surveyed her surroundings. "I wouldn't mind getting a visual on how the whole scene played out."

"Good idea." Delta ran inside the house to grab the keys. When she returned, the trio made their way to the spot where Duke had found Barnaby's body.

Piles of dirt surrounded a gaping hole. Careful not to disturb the site, Jo and Delta showed Raylene the exact spot where Duke had alerted them.

An orange flag, something Jo hadn't noticed before, was sticking out of the ground. "I don't remember seeing that."

"The investigators must've marked the spot." Raylene cautiously stepped closer and studied the area.

"They found Gary's pocket watch near the body, along with some rope that matches rope they found inside the barn."

"Which is where Gary was letting Barnaby stay for a short time."

"Correct." Jo nodded.

Delta jingled the keys. "Let's go check it out."

The proximity from the pump to the barn was mere steps. It would have been fairly easy for someone to bury Barnaby's body since the pump was out of the visual range of Gary's house.

"What's down there?" Raylene pointed to a line of trees off in the distance.

Delta shaded her eyes. "The neighbor's house. I can't remember their names."

"And those are the closest neighbors, besides us."

"Yep. It's one of the reasons Gary loves this place. It's private, and there are no close neighbors." Delta led them to the double set of barn doors.

"I love old barns." Jo ran a light hand across one of the antique iron hinges. "Gary's barn is in great shape."

"It's been standing for decades now." The door creaked loudly as Delta eased it open. "I've been bugging Gary about cleaning it up. The last time we were out here was to install Carrie's engagement gift."

"That's right." Jo chuckled. "The circle of life hawk."

Delta jabbed her finger toward a perch in the peak of the barn ceiling. "I had Gary hoist it up there." She sniffed the mothball scented air. "It's doing a dandy job of keeping the rodents away; I'll give you that."

A wooden ladder leading to the hayloft was off-center and to the left. "From what Gary said, Barnaby was sleeping up there."

Raylene spun in a slow circle. "It wouldn't hurt to have a look around down here, as well."

The women split up. Delta headed left, Raylene going in the opposite direction and Jo searching the center area. They regrouped a short time later.

"It's clean." Raylene dusted her hands.

"Same here," Jo reported.

"Ditto," Delta said.

The trio climbed the ladder, stepping into the loft, which was lined with bales of hay. There was a pulley system anchored in the ceiling's peak, extending all the way down to the cement floor with a large metal hook attached at the end.

Loose hay crunched under Jo's feet as she took a tentative step forward. "Let's split up again."

The women scoured the area and then began inspecting every single bale of hay. Like the main floor, they found nothing even remotely resembling a clue.

Delta shoved a bale of hay against the wall and plopped down. "This was a bust. I kinda figured we wouldn't find anything."

"We had to try." Jo joined her and perched on the edge of the bale of hay. She grimaced as the prickly straw poked her backside. "Nothing ventured, nothing gained."

Raylene leaned her hip against a post. "What did Gary say about Barnaby staying up here?"

"He didn't stay for very long," Delta said. "When Gary found out he was stealing, he kicked him off his property."

"He made a comment Barnaby was anxious to get back in the barn, but Gary wouldn't let him," Jo added.

"Which means he left something of importance up here." Raylene tugged on a stray strand of hair.

"Gary said Barnaby left a bunch of junk, and he tossed it out."

Jo abruptly stood. "I'm at a loss."

Raylene waited for Jo and Delta to descend the stairs. She did an about-face and began backing down.

A beam of bright sunlight glinted through a crack in the barn wall, casting a beacon of light into the hayloft.

Something shiny caught her eye. "Hang on. I think we missed something." Raylene scrambled back up the ladder. A piece of metal was partially tucked behind a loose board. "There's something here."

Jo clambered to the top and joined Raylene. "It's stuck."

Raylene attempted to pry it out, wiggling it back and forth. "Whatever it is – it's wedged in there."

Jo ran to the railing and motioned to Delta. "We need something with a sharp edge. A crowbar would work."

Delta hurried out of the barn. She returned a few moments later and climbed the ladder, joining the others. Jo gripped the small object, while Raylene wedged the flat end of the crowbar under the board and gently pried it up.

"Almost there," Jo said. "It's coming loose."

Seconds later, the shiny metal object dropped into Jo's hand. "It's a key." She handed it to Raylene.

"This is a storage locker key. Check it out. There's a number on the back." She turned to Delta. "Are there any storage facilities around here?"

"One. It's Centerpoint Storage."

Jo's heart skipped a beat. "Finally, maybe we're onto something."

Back at the farm, they made a beeline for Jo's office, where she did a quick online search of area storage companies. Delta was right. There was only one – Centerpoint Storage.

Jo dialed their number and put the call on speaker.

"Centerpoint Storage. Glen speaking."

"Yes. I found a key at a property I'm moving into. It looks like a storage unit key, and since you're the only storage facility in the area, I was wondering if you could verify it."

"I'll try."

Jo described the key and then rattled off the numbers.

"That's one of our keys. The unit was under a one-year lease. The lease expired last month."

Jo's heart plummeted. "I see. So, did the owner pick up the contents?"

More tapping. "Nope. The contents were never claimed."

"What...what happened to them?"

"They're still on site. We send a letter to the last known address and then hold them for ninety days. If, after ninety days, there's no response, we either toss the contents or auction them off."

"Which means you still have the contents of the unit. Can you tell me the renter's name?"

"Unfortunately, I can't because of our privacy policy."

"What about verifying it?" Raylene whispered loudly.

Jo nodded. "What about verifying it – if I were to give you a name?"

There was a moment of silence. "Yeah. Sure. I can do that."

"Barnaby Iteen."

More clicking on the other end. "Yes, ma'am. That was the renter."

Delta let out a faint whoop.

"You're the second person who's called about that unit in the last week."

"Someone else was asking about Mr. Iteen's storage unit?"

"Yeah. Some guy. I didn't catch his name. He wanted to know what happened to the contents of the unit too. I told him what I told you."

"Would it be possible for us to stop to check out what was in there?"

"It's against company policy. You'll need to provide me photo identification, matching the rental agreement if you want me to show you what was in there."

"But I have the key. Surely, that makes a difference. What if I paid the past due fees?" Jo wasn't ready to give up. "And sweetened the pot by giving you a little bonus for helping me out?"

"Bonus?"

"Cash," Jo said bluntly.

"Hmmm...I guess I could make an exception," Glen said. "You said you have the key?"

"It's in my hand." Jo told him she would be there within the hour and hurriedly ended the call before he could change his mind.

She waved the phone in the air. "This key might hold the answer to what happened to Barnaby."

"Before we leave, let's do some digging around into the Half Wall Bar." Jo turned her computer on and typed in Half Wall Bar, Kansas.

The screen filled. Jo double-clicked on the first link and began reading it aloud. It was an article about a brawl in the parking lot. Two bar patrons began fighting. One broke free, climbed into his car and attempted to run over the other patron.

There was also an article about Flo and her now ex-husband's messy divorce. One article even suggested the place was potentially cursed when it suffered heavy damage during a suspicious fire.

The headline of an article near the bottom, one Jo hadn't noticed during her previous search, caught her eye. "Family feud or something sinister?"

Jo clicked on the link. It was another story about the bar's woes, mentioning the suspicious fire and multiple visits by the police. Toward the end, there was a quote from Dexter Parlow. "The family is determined to keep Half Wall Bar, an area landmark, up and running."

"Who is Dexter Parlow?" Delta asked.

"Obviously, someone related to Flo." Jo typed in his name. Information about him popped up, including him being mentioned as co-owner of Half Wall Bar. "I don't think he's Flo's ex-husband."

"Call Miles," Delta suggested. "He's a regular over there."

"Good idea." Jo dialed her brother's number. It went to voice mail. She started to leave a message when his name popped up on the screen. She ended her call and answered his. "Hey, Miles."

"Hey, Jo. What's up?"

Jo briefly filled him in on their visit with Charlie Golden, their search of Gary's barn, the discovery of the key and her online research. "We've been digging around in the Half Wall Bar's history. The name Dexter Parlow popped up. He was mentioned as co-owner of the Half Wall Bar."

"Yeah, Dex. I know him."

"Who is he?"

"Flo's son."

Jo nearly fell out of her chair at what Miles told her next.

Chapter 23

"Now that you mention it, he hadn't been around the bar for a few weeks until yesterday. I saw him when Sherry and I were there. He was limping. Said he fell off his back porch and twisted his ankle."

"Dexter Parlow, a part-owner of Half Wall Bar, hasn't been around for a while. He reappeared yesterday. You noticed he was limping, and he claimed he twisted his ankle after falling off his back porch."

"Yep."

"I think you've helped us narrow down the list of suspects." Jo thanked him and ended the call. "We're onto something."

"What if..." Raylene began to pace. "I want to go over everything, starting from the beginning. Barnaby Iteen, a drifter, blew into town a couple

345

years ago. He did some odd jobs, got into trouble for stealing, including stealing from Gary and at least one other guy."

"Rick Pringle, the owner of Pringle Construction."

"Right. Before things went south, Gary let him camp out in his barn, which is where we found the key to the storage unit. His close friend, Charlie Golden, told you that Barnaby bragged he had something on someone shortly before his disappearance."

Raylene continued. "The bar is having financial difficulties, there's an ugly divorce and it catches on fire."

"Yes, yes and yes."

"Barnaby's hangout is the bar. What if the dirt he has on someone involves the bar?"

"And now there's someone else who's been snooping around, trying to find out what Barnaby had in storage," Jo reminded them.

"Which could be Dexter Parlow," Raylene said. "But how would anyone else know about the storage unit?"

Delta's jaw dropped. "Jo, someone broke into Gary's barn a couple of months ago. We figured it was a bunch of kids messing around."

Jo stared at Delta. "I remember you mentioning it now. According to Charlie, someone has been messing around the chapel, as well."

"Which is another spot where Barnaby hung out. Perhaps Barnaby's killer or killers are desperate to get their hands on whatever he was keeping in a safe place."

"Not so fast." Raylene lifted a hand. "What if it was Charlie Golden?"

"He and Barnaby were friends. He doesn't fit the MO." Jo shook her head. "My money is on Flo's son, Dexter, who also happens to be a part-owner of the bar."

The women discussed the possible list of suspects. Now, all they had to do was visit the storage facility to find out what Barnaby stashed in his unit.

*****

The storage facility, a large, sprawling complex with units for as far as the eye could see, was closer to Smithville than Divine. Jo drove through the open gate and parked near the front office.

The trio exited the vehicle and made their way inside. A bell chimed announcing their arrival. A man in his late thirties emerged from the back and approached the counter. "Good afternoon."

"Good afternoon." Jo greeted him. "Are you Glen?"

"I am."

"I called earlier about a key I found. You told me I could stop by to check out the contents of the storage unit if I paid the past due fees and showed you the key."

"Yes, ma'am."

Jo pulled the key from her pocket and set it on the counter.

Glen picked it up. "Yep. This is one of our keys. I'll need to confirm it's a match for the unit you were asking about." He slipped his glasses on and turned his attention to the computer. "It was for one of our smaller rental units, a five by five." He studied the screen. "Since the lease just ran out and we're less than a month in, it'll be fifty-one dollars and ninety-nine cents."

"Fifty-one bucks for a small box? We're in the wrong business," Delta muttered.

"You're under no obligation to pay the fee."

"No. I'll pay." Jo fumbled inside her purse for her credit card. She waited for him to give the signal and then slid it into the reader. The transaction finished processing. He handed her the receipt, eyeing her expectantly.

"What?"

"I thought we agreed that since I'm bending the rules, you were gonna make it worth my while."

"Right." Jo reached for her wallet.

"I'll take care of this." Delta nudged her aside as she pulled her wallet out. She set a ten-dollar bill on the counter.

He stared at it.

"I gave you ten bucks."

"I'm thinking if you went to all of the trouble of driving over here, whatever was in the unit is worth more than ten bucks."

"Fine." Delta grabbed another ten and set it next to the first.

"Thank you." Glen tucked the bills in his front pocket. "Meet me around the side of the building, beyond the overhead door to the right of the entrance."

The trio trudged out of the building. "That's highway robbery," Delta grumbled. "Makes you wonder how much a larger unit costs."

"I'm almost afraid to ask."

Glen was waiting for them inside the door. He led them across the cavernous expanse to a secured area. He stepped inside and began searching the shelves. "I don't see it anymore."

Jo's heart sank.

"Uh. Hang on. Here it is." He removed two cardboard storage boxes and placed them on a nearby folding table. "These were the only two items inside the unit."

The women gathered around the table, lifting the lid on the first box. It was full of file folders. Jo handed a third of the stack to Raylene, a third to Delta and kept the final third for herself.

Each folder contained a separate job sheet, some for cleanup, some for painting and minor building repairs. Jo flipped through several, but nothing caught her eye.

A buzzer echoed loudly. "I got someone out front. I'll be right back." Glen made his way out of the locked area.

Raylene finished sifting through her stack. "This guy ran some sort of handyman business."

Delta turned her attention to the second container, which was a clear plastic bin. She lifted the lid and removed a small cardboard box.

Jo peered inside. "This is full of tools."

"Maybe they were hot," Raylene suggested.

"Meaning Barnaby was dealing in stolen goods?"

"Hang on." Delta excitedly motioned to them. "I think I might have found something."

Chapter 24

"What is it?" Jo leaned in.

"A handheld recorder." Delta fiddled with the buttons on the side. "It's deader than a doornail." Using her thumb, she slid the cover off, revealing a pair of leaking batteries.

"There's something else." Raylene reached for a file folder that was tucked behind a hand sander. "This one is labeled Half Wall Bar." She flipped it open. Inside were several work orders. "It looks like Barnaby Iteen did some work for Half Wall Bar right after their fire." She let out a low whistle. "I've never hired a handyman before, but this guy's rates were outrageous."

"Let me see that." Jo studied the work order. "You're right. These charges are ridiculous. No one in their right mind would agree to these amounts." There were handwritten notations on the side with payments being made, the date and the dollar amount. "If this information is accurate, Flo still owed Barnaby a substantial amount of money."

Delta held the recorder up. "Something tells me we're gonna wanna hear what's on this."

Jo lowered her voice. "Glen isn't going to let us walk off with this. We'll have to sneak it out."

"I'll hide it." Raylene shoved the recorder in her front pocket.

"Let's take a closer look at Barnaby's notes." Jo studied the bar's work orders that indicated the kitchen drywall and painting had been completed, and there was a handwritten notation about some soot. She removed her cell phone from her pocket and snapped pictures, making sure she captured a clear shot of every detail.

Glen returned a short time later. "Did you find what you were looking for?"

"We did." A sudden thought occurred to Jo. "You said someone else called to inquire about Mr. Iteen's storage unit."

"Yes. It was a man."

"Did he happen to give you his name?"

"Nope. But I have his number."

Jo's heart skipped a beat. "It's important we find out who else was asking about the storage unit."

"How important?"

"Important enough to make it worth your trouble."

Glen's eyes lit. "Well, since you put it like that. I have the number in the office."

The women followed him to the office, watching as he grabbed a sticky note. He jotted a number down and handed it to Jo.

In return, she handed him a twenty. "Thank you."

The women exited the office and returned to the SUV. Jo reached for her seatbelt. "I remember passing a convenience store on our way here. We'll stop there to grab some batteries."

It was a quick trip to the store. Once there, Delta and Raylene waited while Jo ran inside.

When she returned, Delta swapped out the dead batteries for a fresh set. "Here goes nothing." She hit the play button, and they could hear someone talking. "Jackpot." Her finger trembled as she rewound the tape to the beginning.

A man began speaking. "I'm calling you out on this right now, Pabst. You and Dexter. I put my butt on the line by starting the fire."

"And we paid you for it, Barnaby," a second man insisted. "That was the deal."

"The deal was a ten percent cut. You paid me five grand. The bar's insurance policy was for half a million," Barnaby argued.

A third man spoke. "Between the money we already gave you and the ridiculous sums you're charging me for the repairs to the bar, you're getting your money."

"You can more than afford to pay me for my work. As a matter of fact, I think you two need to pay me a lot more to keep my mouth shut. I'm sure the authorities would be interested in knowing what actually went down."

One of the other men replied, but his voice was low, and Jo wasn't able to make out what he said.

"I'll give you forty-eight hours to pay me the other forty grand you owe me."

"And then you leave town," one of the other men chimed in.

"I'll leave town," Barnaby agreed.

There was some discussion about where the trio would meet. The recording abruptly ended, and Jo waved the recorder in the air. "This is it. This is the smoking gun we've been searching for."

"It's time to call Sheriff Franklin."

"And tell him what? We 'borrowed' the recorder?" Raylene wrinkled her nose.

"We have no choice. Sheriff Franklin has to hear this."

Jo tapped the steering wheel thoughtfully. "I have an idea. You call Franklin and ask him to meet us at the storage facility."

At Delta's request, the Smith County Sheriff's Department dispatcher forwarded her call to Franklin. "Sheriff Franklin speaking."

"Hello, Sheriff Franklin. This is Delta Childress. I think I may have information regarding the Barnaby Iteen case you'll find interesting."

There was a moment of silence. "Have you spoken to the other investigators?"

"No. I figured I would talk to you first." Delta told him she was on her way to the storage facility and asked if it was possible for him to meet her there.

"It'll take me a few to get there. If you can hang tight, I'm on my way."

"I'll be waiting."

The sheriff arrived not long after the women. "Looks like you brought the whole posse with you."

"We've been working on Iteen's death." Jo explained how Raylene had found the key wedged behind a board in Gary's barn.

"It looked like a storage unit key," Raylene said. "Since this is the only place around, we gave them a call and found out the key was one of theirs."

Delta picked up and finished filling the sheriff in as she removed the handheld recorder from her purse. "We found this in one of Barnaby's boxes. It's self-explanatory."

The women quietly waited while the sheriff listened to the recording. There was a flicker of emotion near the end when it was obvious Barnaby was blackmailing Sonny Pabst and Dexter Parlow.

"There's also a file folder inside one of the boxes from Barnaby's storage unit with detailed notes on work he did at the bar after it burned," Raylene said.

"Interestingly enough, the man who works at the storage office said someone else called about Barnaby's storage unit." Jo handed him the sticky note with the phone number. "Here's the guy's number."

The sheriff lifted a brow. "How did you get this?"

"By paying the guy who works here." Jo rubbed her thumb and index finger together. "We haven't called it yet. I was thinking maybe you could set up a trap and lure the caller down here."

The sheriff scratched his head. "Joanna Pepperdine, if I didn't know any better, I would say you're hankering for a new job as an amateur sleuth."

"I'm only trying to help a friend. Honestly, this is beyond my skill set," Jo joked. "So, are you going to call the number?"

"I reckon with a little help from the fella inside, we might be able to get to the bottom of Barnaby's death."

The sheriff entered the storage office while the women waited outside. He returned a short time later. "Glen made the call. The guy is on his way. You might be onto something, ladies."

"I'll need to hide my patrol car." The sheriff moved his vehicle to the back of the building. A second, unmarked police car arrived and pulled around back.

The officers made their way into the office as the women climbed inside the SUV to wait. The minutes dragged by. A woman in a minivan pulled into the parking lot. She didn't stop at the office but instead drove around back.

Another vehicle pulled in and parked several car lengths away. Sonny Pabst exited the car and hurried into the office.

"Sonny Pabst. Will you look at that?"

"This is still iffy," Raylene warned. "Unless Sheriff Franklin has something up his sleeve, there's no way he can prove Sonny, or even Dexter, actually killed Barnaby."

"Hopefully, he has a plan." Jo knew something was up when another squad car arrived. Two officers exited the vehicle and entered the office.

"I can't stand it." Jo started to step out when the front door opened. The officers, the last to arrive, accompanied a handcuffed Sonny Pabst out of the building and placed him in the back of the patrol car.

"They got him." Delta gave Raylene a high five and sprang from the vehicle. "Thank you, God."

Sheriff Franklin strode out of the building and met them on the sidewalk. "I kinda figured you were still hanging around."

"How did you get him?" Jo asked.

"Tell you what, I'll show you how this takedown happened." He led them inside. "That, right there, cracked the case." Franklin pointed to a large, black box. "That and the young man behind the desk."

Jo squinted her eyes. "What is it?"

"A shredder."

Raylene cast the sheriff a sideways glance. "Glen let Sonny shred the documents we found."

"He thought he shredded them. As soon as Sonny shredded potential evidence. Bam!" Franklin slapped his hands. "We had him."

"I've never seen anything like it in my life." Glen shook his head in awe. "When I asked him if he wanted to use the shredder for a few extra bucks, he couldn't hand me the money and shred those papers fast enough."

"I'm gonna wait 'til he gets down to the station to play the recorder, right after my men pick Dexter up."

"My money is on Sonny, for sure. Him being an insurance broker – not only would he lose his license, but he could potentially spend time behind bars for insurance fraud."

Jo blinked rapidly. "Hang on. You said Sonny is an insurance broker?"

"Yep. Has been for years. If you hadn't found the recorder, our evidence would be flimsy at best. Something tells me once those men hear their own voices confessing to insurance fraud and arson, they're gonna turn on each other."

*****

It was a couple days later before Jo and Delta heard back from Sheriff Franklin. He stopped by the farm to thank them for helping crack the case.

"So, who was it?" Jo asked.

"Sonny Pabst killed Barnaby and buried him behind Gary's barn. He also named Dexter as his accomplice."

"What about Flo?" Jo asked.

"Both men claim she knew nothing about it. Whether she did or not...we may never know."

According to Franklin, Sonny sold Half Wall Bar a business income insurance policy, also known as business interruption insurance. The bar was in trouble. After Flo's divorce and her ex taking half of everything, she was having difficulty with cash flow.

"So, she figured a business interruption policy would help if anything happened. She bought a policy and voilà." Jo snapped her fingers. "Next thing you know, the place catches fire. Even if Flo wasn't involved, it sounds fishy."

"I agree with you, but, again, Dexter and Sonny both insist she had no idea. She was not caught on tape, nor is there any sign of her involvement."

Franklin shifted his feet. "Dexter, who also negotiated a plea deal for naming Sonny as the killer, confirmed that once Barnaby found out how much the payout was, he blackmailed them. Sonny freaked out, knowing his career was on the line and killed him. Only Barnaby knows if he would've taken the money and run or hung around looking for more."

"And dead men don't talk," Delta said. "Why involve Gary by burying Barnaby's body on his property?"

"Because Gary had motive and opportunity. Divine is a small town. I'm sure most people knew about Gary's troubles with Barnaby, not to mention the fact Barnaby had been staying in Gary's barn."

"I suspected it might have been Rick Pringle, a bar regular, who had assaulted Barnaby not long before his disappearance," Jo said.

Franklin tilted his head, eyeing Jo with interest. "You were on this case."

"I knew Gary wasn't responsible and wanted to help him and Delta since we heard the authorities were close to making an arrest. We can't have Gary in jail when he should be walking down the aisle."

"Gary wasn't going to jail, at least not yet. He was a suspect, but so were Rick Pringle and Charlie Golden."

Delta told him about the incident some months back where someone had broken into the barn. "Could be Sonny or even Dexter was looking for whatever dirt Barnaby had on them."

"Stands to reason, which could also be why Charlie Golden and the Centerpoint Chapel have been targeted recently, as well," the sheriff said. "How did you say you found the storage unit key?"

"It was our resident, Raylene. She helped search the barn. On her way down from the hayloft, the sun happened to hit the key *just* right."

"Perhaps it was a Divine Intervention."

"I wouldn't be surprised if we had a little help." Jo smiled. "This farm and its residents have had more than their share of miracles."

Chapter 25

"It's hotter than blazes." Delta snatched a magazine off the coffee table and began fanning her face. "Whose idea was it to get married on one of the hottest days of the year?"

"Yours," Jo and Sherry said in unison.

"And Gary's," Kelli chimed in.

"You're a beautiful bride. Besides, the porch is shaded, and we've installed some portable air conditioning units in the barn to keep it cool," Jo said.

"Is Gary here?" Delta bustled over to the window and lifted the corner of the curtain. "He's not here. He's probably gonna back out."

"He's not backing out." Jo chuckled. "He's in Nash's apartment getting ready. I watched him go up there."

"Okay. Good. Good." Delta sucked in a breath. "What about the food?"

"Marlee has it all under control, and Laverne is putting the finishing touches on the cake."

"Pastor Murphy?" Delta snatched a tissue from the box and began dabbing her forehead.

"He's on his way. In fact, there he is now." Jo met him at the door and ushered him inside.

"You've got quite a crowd out there," the pastor said. "Where's our bride?"

"Over here." Delta began fanning her face even faster. "I'm having trouble breathing. I hope I don't pass out."

"You'll be fine." Pastor Murphy lightly touched her arm. "We'll have you and Gary married before you know it. As a matter of fact, I think it's time to get started."

"Nash and Gary are here." Jo slipped onto the porch and turned the radio on. The pre-wedding music started as the men took their places. Nash caught Jo's eye and winked.

Poor Gary was visibly trembling as he clutched a cloth handkerchief. Pastor Murphy stepped outside, taking his place next to the men.

One by one, Delta's bridesmaids, Kelli, Leah, Michelle, Raylene and Sherry, waltzed out of the house and onto the porch. Jo was last. She gave Delta a gentle hug and handed her a beautiful bouquet of pink roses. "You look stunning. Gary is a lucky guy."

"Thanks, Jo."

Jo cast her friend one final glance before stepping onto the porch and taking her place on the front steps.

The wedding march began playing as Delta slowly made her way along the porch. She joined Gary and Pastor Murphy while Nash discreetly stepped back.

Delta and Gary had unanimously decided on short and sweet vows. After finishing, the crowd sprang to their feet and applauded. They whistled, hooted and hollered as Gary kissed his bride.

Delta triumphantly lifted her bouquet and let out a whoop of her own.

Gary proudly offered his wife his arm as they strolled to the other end of the porch and down the steps where the bridesmaids, along with Nash and Jo, took turns hugging them.

The guests waited until the wedding party passed by before following behind.

Delta's niece, Patti, was there. So were Gary's children and grandchildren. Marlee hugged the couple and then hurried off to take care of the final details.

Carrie bustled over, sporting a hot pink hat with a bird of paradise tucked along the edge. "This was absolutely *the* most fab wedding ever."

She hugged Gary and then Delta. "I thought for a minute, there, you were gonna hit the floor, Delta."

"Me too."

"I better get going. I offered to give Marlee a hand with the food." Carrie tottered off and was replaced by others who were eager to congratulate the couple.

Gary and Delta beamed as the well-wishers surrounded them. The guests began making their way to the barn while Claire, who had offered to take the wedding pictures, corralled the wedding party.

After finishing, they joined the guests. The food, fun and festivities were soon underway. The residents all pitched in to help Laverne assemble the wedding cake, which had turned out beautifully.

Laverne beamed as Delta and Gary oohed and aahed over it, thanking her for making it.

The portable air conditioning units kept the barn bearable, and when the quartet showed up, the makeshift dance floor filled. Daylight faded, and the twinkle lights Nash and Gary had installed cast a romantic glow inside the barn.

Some of the guests had left, but quite a few still remained. The quartet announced last call for drinks and dancing. Jo grabbed a trash bag and began making her rounds when she felt a light tap on her shoulder.

She turned to find Nash standing behind her. "You've been buzzing around here like a bee, and I haven't had a chance to ask you for a dance. May I?" He reached for Jo's hand.

"Yes, you may."

Nash waited for her to set the bag down and then led her onto the dance floor, where he pulled her into his arms. They swayed to the music, and she closed her eyes. Around and around, they went until the final notes faded away.

She lifted her head and found him gazing at her with an unrecognizable look in his eyes. "You look beautiful tonight."

"And you're so handsome; it takes my breath away," she whispered.

He tightened his grip. "You're officially an empty-nester now."

Jo grinned. "Yes, I suppose you could say that."

"It's a big house for just one woman. Maybe someday down the road, you wouldn't mind sharing it again with someone," he hinted.

Jo's breath caught in her throat as their eyes met. "I suppose I might be open to the idea of sharing my home with someone."

"That's what I was hoping you would say." Nash lowered his head, claiming her lips in a kiss that made Jo forget everything else.

The end.

If you enjoyed reading "Divine Wedding," would you please take a moment to leave a review? It would mean so much. Thank you! – Hope

The Divine Mystery Series Continues!

Book 8, coming soon!

Read the Complete Series:

Divine Intervention: Book 1
Divine Secrets: Book 2
Divine Blindside: Book 3
Divine Decisions: Book 4
Divine Christmas: Book 5
Divine Courage: Book 6
Divine Wedding: Book 7
Divine Cozy Mystery Book 8 (Coming Soon!)

Read More by Hope
(Click Links Below To Buy or Read FREE with
Kindle Unlimited)

Garden Girls Cozy Mystery Series
*A lonely widow finds new purpose for her life when she
and her senior friends help solve a murder in their
small Midwestern town.*

Garden Girls - The Golden Years
The brand new spin-off series of the Garden Girls
Mystery series! You'll enjoy the same fun-loving
characters as they solve mysteries in the cozy town
of Belhaven. Each book will focus on one of the
Garden Girls as they enter their "golden years."

Divine Cozy Mystery Series

*After relocating to the tiny town of Divine, Kansas,
strange and mysterious things begin to happen to
businesswoman, Jo Pepperdine and those around her.*

Cruise Ship Cozy Mystery Series
*A recently divorced senior lands her dream job as
Assistant Cruise Director onboard a mega passenger
cruise ship and soon discovers she's got a knack for
solving murders.*

Samantha Rite Mystery Series

Heartbroken after her recent divorce, a single mother is persuaded to book a cruise and soon finds herself caught in the middle of a deadly adventure. Will she make it out alive?

Made in Savannah Cozy Mystery Series
A mother and daughter try to escape their family's NY mob ties by making a fresh start in Savannah, GA but they soon realize you can run but you can't hide from the past.

Sweet Southern Sleuths Short Stories Series
Twin sisters with completely opposite personalities become amateur sleuths when a dead body is discovered in their recently inherited home in Misery, Mississippi.

Italian Chicken Rollup Recipe

<u>Ingredients</u>:

4 boneless skinless chicken breasts – sliced in half (approx. 4 oz. each)

12 pepperoni slices

¼ cup chopped green olives (optional)

10-12 pieces of thinly-sliced red onion

8 slices Italian cheese (or mozzarella)

1 15 oz. jar pizza sauce

<u>Directions</u>:

-Preheat oven to 350 degrees F.

-Flatten chicken to ¼ inch thickness (or buy thinly-sliced chicken breast cutlets).

-Place 3 pepperoni slices on one end of each chicken breast.

- Evenly place divided chopped green olives and red onion on top of pepperoni.

-Top each chicken breast with 1 slice of cheese.

-Starting at end with topping, roll up tightly.

-Secure with toothpicks, one on each end of each roll-up.

-Place in greased 11x7 inch glass baking dish.

-Spoon pizza sauce on top.

-Cover and bake for 35-40 minutes or until chicken reaches internal temperature of 165 degrees F.

-Remove from oven. Uncover. Top with remaining cheese.

-Bake for an additional five minutes or until cheese is melted.

-Or optional broiling for 1-2 minutes or until cheese is lightly browned.

Laverne's Lucky 7 Layer Burrito Recipe

<u>Ingredients</u>:

1 15 oz. can refried beans

Small amount extra-virgin olive oil

4 finely chopped scallions

1 8 oz. can of sweet corn

2 tbsp. chopped cilantro

1 cup chipotle salsa

1 15 oz. can black beans

Ground cumin to taste

2 cups sour cream

1 lime, juiced

2 ripe avocados, cubed and lightly mashed.

2 cloves garlic, finely chopped

Salt to taste

2 plum tomatoes, diced

Diced lettuce

9 inch soft tortillas

Tortilla chips

Directions:

-Heat refried beans in small saucepan over medium heat.

-After heating, spread beans in bottom of medium, deep-dish glass bowl.

-Scrape pan and return to heat.

-Heat corn in pan. Spread over top of refried beans.

-Using now empty pan, turn heat on high. Add small amount of EVOO (extra-virgin olive oil). Add scallion and sear.

-Add chipotle salsa. Heat thoroughly.

-Pour mixture evenly over top of corn.

-Return pan to heat. Add drained black beans.

-Heat thoroughly.

-Add cumin. Season as desired.

-Stir thoroughly.

-Scoop black beans on top of chipotle salsa. Spread evenly.

-Chill in fridge until slightly firm.

-While beans are chilling, combine sour cream and lime juice in medium dish. Set aside.

-In another bowl, combine meat of two mashed avocados, with garlic and salt (to taste).

-Remove chilled beans from fridge.

-Line counter with soft tortillas.

-Spread even amount of slightly chilled bean mixture along center of tortilla.

-Roll tortilla, place on large plate. Repeat until all tortillas are filled.

-Spread sour cream/lime mixture across top of each wrapped burrito.

-Top each with diced tomatoes and lettuce.

-Garnish top of each burrito with guacamole.

-Serve with a side of salsa and tortilla chips.

Order of burrito layers:

1. Refried beans
2. Corn
3. Chipotle salsa
4. Black beans
5. Sour cream and lime juice mixture (on top)
6. Garnish of diced tomatoes and lettuce (on top)
7. Top with guacamole (on top)

Made in the USA
Thornton, CO
07/15/23 13:08:58

1cf547e9-9583-4aef-bccc-a563c46ca25aR01